from
First Crossing

Stories by

Pam Muñoz Ryan
Lensey Namioka
Elsa Marston
Minfong Ho

HAMPTON-BROWN

THE EXCHANGE

Does every problem have a solution?

Hampton-Brown
P.O. Box 223220
Carmel, California 93922
800-333-3510
www.hampton-brown.com

Printed in the United States of America

ISBN-13: 978-0-7362-2813-8
ISBN-10: 0-7362-2813-6

09 10 11 12 13 14 10 9 8 7 6 5 4

CONTENTS

First Crossing

Pam Muñoz Ryan

Marco's father has crossed the border into the United States illegally several times to make money to support his family in Mexico. Now it is Marco's turn to make the dangerous journey.

First Crossing

Pam Muñoz Ryan

Revolution Boulevard in downtown Tijuana **swarmed with gawking tourists** who had walked over the big cement bridge from the United States to Mexico. Shop owners stood in front of their stalls calling out, "I make you good deal. Come in. I make you good price." Even though it was January, children walked the streets barefooted and **accosted** shoppers, determined to sell gum and small souvenirs with their persistent pleas: "Come on, lady, you like gum? Chiclets? Everybody like gum." Vendors carried gargantuan bouquets of paper flowers,

....

swarmed with gawking tourists was filled with people visiting the city

accosted bothered

hurrying up to cars on the street and trying to **make sales** through open windows. It appeared that no one ever accepted the first rebuff from tourists. The Mexicans simply badgered them until they pulled out their wallets. With its shady, border-town reputation, Tijuana **maintained an undeniable sense of mystery, as if something illegal was about to transpire**.

Marco added up the hours he'd been riding on buses from his home in Jocotepec, Jalisco, in order to reach Tijuana. Eighteen hours? Twenty-three hours? It was all a blur of sleeping and sitting in stations and huddling as close to his father as possible so he wouldn't have to smell the sweat of strangers. Now, even though they were finally in the **border town**, their journey still wasn't over. Papá pointed to a bench in front of a store, and Marco gratefully dropped onto it. Even though it wasn't dark yet, neon signs flashed in the store window. Marco felt conscious of himself, as if everyone who passed by knew why he was there. For some reason he felt guilty, even though he hadn't yet done anything wrong.

....

make sales sell things

maintained an undeniable sense of mystery, as if something illegal was about to transpire was a strange place where people did bad things

border town place where many people crossed the border between Mexico and the United States

"*No te apures.* Don't worry," said Papá, reaching into a brown bag for a peanut. He calmly cracked and peeled it, letting the shells drop on the sidewalk.

Marco looked at him. Papá had an eagle's profile: a brown bald head with a bird-of-prey nose. Once, when he was a little boy, Marco had seen a majestic carved wooden Indian in front of a store in Guadalajara and had said, "Papá, that's you!" Papá had laughed but had to agree that the statue looked familiar. Marco looked just like Papá but with **ten times the** hair. They had the same walnut-colored skin and hooked noses, but Papá's body was muscular and firm while Marco's was skinny and angular, all knees and elbows.

"How do we find the *coyote*?" asked Marco.

"Do not worry," said Papá. "The *coyote* will find us. Like a real animal **stalking** its next meal, the *coyote* will find us."

Marco took off his baseball cap and ran his fingers through his thick, straight hair. He repositioned the hat and took a deep breath. "Papá, what happens if we get caught?"

....

ten times the a lot more

coyote person who will bring us to the United States

stalking looking for

"**We have been over this**," said Papá, still cracking peanuts. "We will have to spend a few hours at the border office. We stand in line. They ask us questions. We give them the names we discussed. They take our fingerprints. Then we come back here to Tijuana. The *coyote* will try to move us across again, tomorrow or the next day or even the next. It could take two attempts or a dozen. Eventually, we make it. It's all part of the fee."

"How much?" asked Marco.

"Too much," said Papá. "**It is how it is.** They are greedy, but we need them."

Marco had heard stories about *coyotes*, the men who moved Mexicans across the border. Sometimes they took the money from poor peasants, disappeared, and left them stranded in Nogales or Tecate with no way home. *Coyotes* had been known to lead groups into the desert in the summer, where they would later be found almost dead and **riddled with** cactus thorns. And then there were the stories about scorpion stings and rattlesnake bites after following a *coyote* into a dry riverbed. Just last week, Marco overheard a friend of Papá's tell about a group of people who hid in a truck under a camper shell, bodies

....

We have been over this We already talked about what will happen

It is how it is. That is the way things happen.

riddled with full of

9

piled upon bodies. The **border patrol** tried to stop the truck, but the *coyote* was drunk and tried to speed away. The truck overturned, and seventeen Mexicans were killed. Since then, **Marco's thoughts had been filled with his worst imaginings**.

Papá saw the wrinkle in Marco's forehead and said, "I have always **made it across**, and I wouldn't keep doing this if it wasn't worth it."

Marco nodded. Papá was right. Everything had been better for the family since he'd started crossing. His father had not always worked in the United States. For many years, before Marco was ten, Papá had gone to work at a large construction site in Guadalajara, thirty miles away from their village of Jocotepec. Six days a week, Papá had carried fifty-pound bags of rock and dirt from the bottom of a **crater** to the top of the hill. All day long, up and down the hill.

Marco had asked him once, "Do you count the times you go up and down the hill?"

Papá had said, "I don't count. I don't think. I just do it."

....

border patrol police officers who guarded the border
Marco's thoughts had been filled with his worst imaginings Marco worried that bad things would happen
made it across crossed the border without a problem
crater big hole

Papa's frustration had grown as the years went by. He **was nothing more than** a *burro*. When the hole in the ground was dug and the big building finished, he had been sent to excavate another hole. And for what? A pitiful five dollars for his nine hours? The day that one of *los jefes* spat on his father as if he was an animal, Papá set the fifty-pound bag down and began to walk away.

The bosses laughed at him. "Where are you going? You need work? You better stay!"

Papá turned around and picked up the heavy bag. He stayed for the rest of the day so that he could collect his pay and get a ride home, but he never went back.

He told Mamá, "My future and the children's future **are marked in stone here**. Why not go to the other side? There, I will make thirty, forty, fifty dollars a day, maybe more."

For the past four years, Marco had seen Papá only twice a year. He and his mother and younger sisters had **moved into another rhythm of existence**. He woke with the roosters, went to school in the mornings, and helped Mamá with Maria, Lilia, and Irma in the afternoon.

....

was nothing more than felt like
are marked in stone here will never get better if I stay here
moved into another rhythm of existence learned to live without Papá

During harvest, he worked in the corn or *chayote* fields and counted the days until Papá would come home.

The money orders always preceded him. They made Mamá happy and made Papá seem godlike in her eyes. They still did not own a house, but now they were able to pay the rent on time and had plenty left over for things like a television and the clothes and games Marco's sisters always wanted. They had money for the market and food, especially for the occasions when Papá came home and Mamá cooked meat and sweets every day. The first few nights were always the same. Mamá made *birria*, goat stew, and *capirotada*, bread pudding. Then Papá went out with his *compadres* to tell them of his work in Los Estados, the states. The family would **have his company** for a month, and then he would go back to that unknown place, disappearing somewhere beyond the vision of the departing bus.

"What is it like, Papá?" Marco always asked.

"I live in an apartment above a garage with eight messy men. We get up early, when it's still dark, to start our work in the flower fields. In the afternoon, we go back to the apartment. We take turns going to the store to buy

....

The money orders always preceded him. He always sent money before he came home.

have his company live with him

tortillas, a little meat, some fruit. There is a television, so we watch the Spanish stations. We talk about sports and Mexico and our families. There is room on the floor to sleep. On weekends we sometimes play *fútbol* at the school. Sometimes we have regular work, but other times we go and stand on the corner in front of the gas station with the hope we will be picked up by the contractors who need someone to dig a ditch or do some other job **a *gringo*** won't do. It goes on like this until it's time to come back to Mexico."

For several years, Marco had begged to go with Papá. His parents finally decided that now that he was fourteen, he was old enough to help support the family. With both Marco and Papá working, the family could buy a house next year. Mamá had cried for three days before they left.

When it was time to board the bus to Guadalajara, Marco had hugged his mother tight.

"Mamá, I will be back."

"It will never be the same," she'd said. "Besides, some come back and some do not."

Marco knew he would return. He already looked forward to his first homecoming, when he would be

....

a *gringo* an American (in Spanish)

13

celebrated like Papá. As the bus pulled away from Jocotepec, Marco had waved out the small window to the women, and for the first time in his life, had felt like a man.

BEFORE YOU MOVE ON...

1. **Summarize** What did Marco and his father plan to do in Tijuana? How did Marco feel about this?

2. **Cause and Effect** Reread page 11. Why did Papá decide to live and work in the United States?

LOOK AHEAD Read pages 15–24 to find out if the travelers get across the border.

Marco leaned back on the hard bench on the Tijuana street and closed his eyes. He already missed Jocotepec and his sisters playing in the corn fields behind the house. He even missed the annoying neighbor's dog barking and Mamá's voice waking him too early for **mass** on Sunday morning when he wanted to sleep.

Papá nudged him. "Stay close to me," he said, grabbing Marco's shirtsleeve.

Marco sat up and looked around. There was nothing unusual happening on the street. What had Papá seen?

A **squat, full** woman wrapped in a red shawl came down the sidewalk with a determined walk. Marco thought her shape resembled a small Volkswagen. Her blue-black hair was pulled back into a tight doughnut on the top of her head, not one strand out of place. Heavy makeup hid her face like a painted mask, and her red mouth was set in a straight line. As she passed, she glanced at Papá and gave a quick nod.

"Let's go," he said.

"That's the *coyote*?" said Marco. "But it is a woman."

"Shhh," said Papá. "Follow me."

Papá **weaved** between the tourists on the street,

....

mass church
squat, full short, heavy
weaved moved

keeping the marching woman in his sight. She pulled out a beeping cell phone and talked into it, then turned off the main avenue and headed deeper into the town's neighborhood. Others seemed to **fall in** with Papá and Marco from doorways and bus stops until they were a group of eight: five men and three women. Up ahead, the *coyote* woman waited at a wooden gate built into the middle of a block of apartments. She walked in and the **little parade** followed her. They continued through a dirty *callejón* between two buildings, **picking their way** around garbage cans until they reached a door in the alley wall.

"In there," she ordered.

Marco followed Papá inside. It seemed to be a small basement with plaster walls and a cement floor. Narrow wooden stairs led up one wall to someplace above. A light bulb with a dangling chain hung in the middle of the room, and in a corner was a combination television and video player with stacks of children's videotapes on the floor. The woman came inside, shut the door, and bolted it. The men and women turned to face her.

"Twelve hundred for each, American dollars," she said.

....

fall in come to walk

little parade line of people

picking their way walking carefully

Twelve hundred for each, American dollars Each person must pay 1,200 American dollars

16

Marco almost choked. He looked around at the others, who appeared to be peasants like him and Papá. Where would they have gotten that kind of money? And how could Papá pay twenty-four hundred dollars for the two of them to cross the border?

The **transients** reached into their pockets for wallets, rolled up pant legs to get to small leather bags strapped around their legs, unzipped inside pouches of jackets, and were soon counting out the bills. Stacks of money appeared. The *coyote* walked to each person, wrote his or her name in a notebook, and collected the fees. Papá counted out 120 bills, all twenties, into her chubby palm.

In his entire life, Marco had never seen so much money in one room.

"*Escucha*. Listen. **Since September 11**, I have had trouble trying to get people across with false documents," she said, "so we will cross in the desert. I have vans and drivers to help. We'll leave in the middle of the night. If you need to **relieve yourself**, use the alley. The television does not work, only the video." Her cell phone beeped again. She put it to her ear and listened as she walked up the stairs, which groaned and creaked under her weight.

....

transients travelers; people who were going to the U.S.

Since September 11 After the U.S. was attacked by terrorists on September 11, 2001

relieve yourself go to the bathroom

Marco heard a door close and a bolt latch.

It was almost dark. Marco and Papá found a spot on the concrete floor near the video player. Marco put his backpack behind him and leaned against it, protecting himself from the soiled wall, where probably hundreds of backs had rested.

One of the women, who was about Mamá's age, smiled at Marco. The others, tired from their travels, settled on the floor and tried to maneuver their bags for support. No one said much. There was murmuring between people sitting close to each other, but **despite the obligatory polite nods, anxiety prevented too much interaction.**

A man next to Papá spoke quietly to him. His name was Javier, and he'd been crossing for twelve years. He had two lives, he said: one in the United States and one in his village in Mexico. The first few years of working in the States, he dreamed of the days he would go home to Mexico and his family, but now he admitted that he sometimes **dreaded his trips back**. He wanted to bring his wife and children with him to work and live in the U.S., but they wouldn't come. Now he went home only

....

despite the obligatory polite nods, anxiety prevented too much interaction people felt too nervous to talk

dreaded his trips back did not want to return to Mexico

once a year. What worried him was that he was starting to **prefer his life on the other side to** his life in Mexico.

Papá nodded as if he understood Javier.

Marco said nothing because he knew that Papá was just being polite. He would never prefer the United States to Mexico.

Marco was too nervous to sleep. He reached over and took several videotapes from the pile. They were all cartoon musicals, luckily in Spanish. He put one in the machine, *The Lion King*, and turned the volume down low. Trancelike, he watched the lion, Simba, lose his father.

"*Hakuna matata*," sang the characters on the video. "No worries."

A series of thoughts paraded through Marco's mind. The desert. Snakes. The possibility of being separated from Papá. Talking with the men in Jocotepec after eating goat stew. A woman *coyote*. Scorpions. He closed his eyes, and **the music in the video became the soundtrack of his piecemeal nightmare**.

....

prefer his life on the other side to like his life in the United States better than

A series of thoughts paraded through Marco's mind. Marco thought of many things.

the music in the video became the soundtrack of his piecemeal nightmare he heard the music in his dreams

Hours later, Papá woke Marco. "Now, *M'ijo*. Let's go."

Marco, jarred from sleep, let Papá pull him up. He rubbed his eyes and tried to focus on the others, who headed out the door.

A man with a flashlight waited until they all gathered in a **huddle**. He wore all black, including his cap, the brim pulled down so far that all that was **apparent** was his black moustache and a small, narrow chin.

They picked their way through the alley again, following the direction of the man's light. At the street, a paneled van waited, the motor running. The door slid open, and Marco could see that the seats had been removed to create a cavern. It was already filled with people, all standing up. Men and women held small suitcases and had plastic garbage bags next to them filled with their belongings.

There didn't seem to be an inch of additional space until the flashlight man yelled, "*¡Mueva!*" Move.

The people in the van crammed closer together as each of the group of eight climbed inside.

"*¡Más!*" said Flashlight Man. The people tried to

....

M'ijo my son (in Spanish)
huddle small group
apparent showing
¡Más! More! (in Spanish)

squash together. Papá jumped inside and grabbed Marco's hand, pulling him in, too, but Marco was still half out. The man shoved Marco as if he were packing an already stuffed suitcase. The others groaned and complained. The doors slid shut behind Marco. When the van **surged** forward, no one fell because there was no room to fall. Their bodies nested together, faces pressed against faces, like tightly **bundled stalks** of celery. Marco turned his head to avoid his neighbor's breath and found his nose pressed against another's ear.

The van headed east for a half hour. Then it stopped suddenly, the door slid open, and Flashlight Man directed them into the night. His cell phone rang to the tune of "Take Me Out to the Ballgame," and he quickly answered it.

"One hour. We will be there," he said into the phone. Then he turned to the small army of people and said, "Let your eyes adjust to the night. Then follow me."

Marco and Papá held back. They were the last in the group forming the line of obedient lambs walking over a hill and down into **an arroyo**. There was no water at

....

surged moved
bundled stalks tied pieces
an arroyo a creek

the bottom—just rocks, dirt, and dry grasses. **Visions of reptiles crowded Marco's mind.** He was relieved when they climbed back up and continued to walk over the mostly barren ground. They crossed through a chainlink fence where an opening had been cut.

"Are we in the United States?" asked Marco.

"Yes," said Papá. "Keep walking."

They walked along a dirt road for another half hour, and in the distance, headlights blinked. Flashlight Man punched a number into his cell phone. The headlights came on again.

"That's it," said Flashlight Man, and they all hurried toward the van, where they were again sandwiched together inside.

That wasn't so bad, thought Marco, as the van sped down a dirt road. **A tiny bud of relief began to flower in his mind.** No worries.

Within five minutes, the van slowed to a crawl and then stopped. Marco heard someone outside barking orders at the driver. Suddenly, the van door slid open and Marco met **La Migra.**

....

Visions of reptiles crowded Marco's mind. Marco was afraid that he would see lizards and snakes.

A tiny bud of relief began to flower in his mind. He started to feel better.

La Migra the immigration officers who guard the border

Four border-patrol officers with guns drawn ordered them out and herded them into two waiting vans with long bench seats. *A small consolation*, thought Marco. They rode back to the border-patrol station in silence. Inside, it was exactly as Papá had said. They stood in line, gave false names during a short interview, were fingerprinted, and released.

"Now what?" asked Marco, as they stood in front of the border-patrol building on the Mexico side.

"We walk back to *la casa del coyote*," said Papá.

It was seven in the morning as they walked down the narrow streets. Most shops weren't open yet, and bars and fences enclosed the vendors' stalls, which were filled with piñatas, leather goods, ceramics, and sombreros. Papá bought premade burritos and Cokes inside a corner *tienda* before they turned down the street that led to Coyote Lady's house.

Many of their group had already **found their way back** to the basement room off the alley. Papá and Marco found a spot against the wall and fell asleep. They woke late in the afternoon, went to the taco vendor on the corner for

....

A small consolation   At least there's a bench
la casa del coyote   the coyote's house (in Spanish)
found their way back   returned

food, and came back and watched the video *The Little Mermaid*.

Marco listened to the fish maiden's song. She wanted to be free to go to another world. *Like me*, he thought. It seemed *everyone* wanted to get to the other side.

In the middle of the night, they were **roused** and put in a van for another attempt to cross over. Again, the border patrol **sat in wait and ambushed them**, as if they had known they were coming. Each night the van took them a little farther east into the desert, but after five attempts, they were no farther into the United States than they'd been the first night.

....

roused woken up; awakened

sat in wait and ambushed them hid and waited to catch them

BEFORE YOU MOVE ON...

1. **Plot** How did the travelers try to cross the border? What happened?

2. **Character** How did Coyote Lady and Flashlight Man treat the Mexican travelers? What does this show about them?

LOOK AHEAD Read pages 25–31 to find out if the Coyote Lady has a new plan for crossing the border.

Early Sunday morning, Coyote Lady came down the stairs into the basement room. She wore a dress like the ones Marco's mother wore for church, a floral print with a white collar, although it was much bigger than any dress his mother owned. Her face was scrubbed clean of makeup, and she looked like someone's aunt or a neighborhood woman who might go to mass every day.

"Today is a big football game, professional, in San Diego. La Migra will be eager to get people into the U.S. in time for the game. We start moving you in one hour, one at a time. The wait will not be bad at the border this morning. But later today, closer to game time, it will be *horrible*."

Marco looked at Papá. He did not want to be separated from him.

Papá said, "How?"

"In a car," said Coyote Lady. "We hide you. If I take only one across at a time, the car doesn't **ride low in the back** and **does not look suspicious**. I drive in a different lane each time. As you can see, we are having trouble with the usual ways, so we try this. It has worked before, especially on a busy day."

----

ride low in the back go down like it does when a lot of people ride in it

does not look suspicious looks like all the other cars

Marco didn't like the idea of being away from Papá. What would happen if Papá got across and he didn't? Or what if he couldn't find Papá on the other side? Then what would he do? He didn't like this part of the journey. Suddenly, he wished he'd stayed home another year in Jocotepec.

As if reading his mind, Papá said, "I will go before you, Marco. And I will wait for you. I will not leave until you arrive. And if you don't arrive, I will come back to Tijuana."

Marco nodded.

Coyote Lady **gave orders** and told a woman to get ready to go. Every hour she stuck her head inside the room and called out another person.

Papá and Marco were the last of the group to go. They walked outside.

In the alley, the trash cans had been pushed aside to make room for an old car, a sedan. Flashlight Man waited beside the car, but he wasn't wearing his usual black uniform. Instead he had on jeans, a blue-and-white football jersey, and a Chargers cap. He lifted the hood.

Inside, a small rectangular coffee table had been placed next to the motor, forming a narrow ledge. Two of

....

gave orders told everyone what to do

the wooden legs disappeared into the **bowels** of the car and two of the legs had been cut short and now provided the braces against the radiator and motor.

"Okay," he said. "You lie down in here. It only takes a half hour. There is a van waiting for you in Chula Vista that will take you to your destinations."

Papá climbed up. Flashlight Man positioned his feet and legs so they would not touch the motor. Papa put his head and upper body on the tiny tabletop, curling his body to make it smaller. For an instant before the hood was closed, Papá's eyes caught Marco's.

Marco turned away so he wouldn't have to see his father **humbled in this manner**.

"*Vámanos*," said Coyote Lady, and she wedged into the driver's seat. Flashlight Man sat on the passenger side. A Chargers football banner and blue pompoms sat on the dashboard as further proof of their deception. The car backed out of the alley and left. Marco closed the gate behind them.

He paced up and down the alley. They had said it would take an hour **roundtrip. The minutes crawled by.**

....

bowels inside
humbled in this manner looking small and unimportant
Vámanos Let's go (in Spanish)
roundtrip to go there and come back
The minutes crawled by. It seemed to take a long time.

Why did Papá agree to do this? Why did he **resign himself to these people**? "It is the way it is," Papá had said. Marco went back into the basement room and walked in circles.

After one hour, he put in a tape, *Aladdin*, and tried to pay attention as the characters sang about a whole new world. It was so easy in the video to get on a flying carpet to reach a magical place. *Where is this new world? Where is Papá? Did he get through?* Marco had never once heard a story of someone crossing over under the hood of a car. He tried to imagine being inside, next to the engine. His stomach **churned**. *Where is my magic carpet?*

The door opened suddenly. Flashlight Man was back. "Let's go," he said.

The car was already positioned in the alley with the hood up. Coyote Lady took Marco's backpack and threw it in the trunk. Marco climbed up on the bumper and swung his legs over the motor, then sat on the **makeshift ledge**. Flashlight Man arranged Marco's legs as if he were in a running position, one leg up, knee bent. One leg straighter, but slightly bent. Marco slowly lowered himself onto his side and put his head on the tabletop. Then he crossed his arms around his chest and watched the sunlight disappear to a tiny crack as the hood was closed.

....

resign himself to these people do what these people said
churned hurt
makeshift ledge ledge made from the table top

"Don't move in there," said Flashlight Man.

Don't worry, thought Marco. **My fear will not permit me to move.**

The motor started. The noise hurt his ears, and within minutes it was hot. The smell of motor oil and gasoline accosted his nostrils. He breathed through his mouth, straining his lips toward the slit where the light crept through for fresh air. The car moved along for about ten minutes until they reached the lanes of traffic that led to the border crossing. Then it was stop and go. Stop and go. Marco's legs began to cramp, but he knew not to move one inch. He tried not to imagine what would happen if he rolled onto the **inner workings** of the car.

The car lurched and stopped, over and over. Marco wanted to close his eyes, but he was afraid that he would get dizzy or disoriented. He watched the small crack between the car and hood **as if it were his lifeline**. A flash of color **obliterated** his line of sunlight as a flower vendor stopped in front of the car, trying to make one last sale to those in the car next to them. "*¡Flores, flores!* You buy cheap!"

....

My fear will not permit me to move. *I am too scared to move.*

inner workings engine

as if it were his lifeline as if it was the thing keeping him alive

obliterated blocked out

The line of cars started to move again, but the flower vendor continued to walk in front of their car. Coyote Lady pressed on the horn. Marco's body trembled as the sound **reverberated** through his body. He inched his hands up to cover his ears. The vendor stepped out of the way, and the car began to move faster.

Marco never knew when they actually crossed the line. He only knew when the car began to speed up on the **freeway**. His body pulsed with the vibrations of the car. Afraid to close his eyes, he watched beads of moisture move across the radiator, as if they had the ability to dance. Marco could not feel his right foot. It had fallen asleep. **Panic crept into his chest and seized his muscles.** He slowly pressed his hand back and forth across his chest to relieve the tightness. "No worries," he whispered. "No worries."

The car stopped and shook with a door being slammed. Marco heard someone fiddling with the hood latch. Light streamed into his eyes, and he squinted. Flashlight Man pulled him from the car and handed over his backpack. Marco stumbled from his dead foot, and his

....

reverberated vibrated

freeway highway

Panic crept into his chest and seized his muscles. He was so scared that he could not move.

body still rocked with the feeling of the moving car. He looked around. He was in a parking lot behind an auto shop. Papá was waiting.

"**We made it**," said Papá, clapping Marco on the back. "We're in Chula Vista."

....

We made it We are here

BEFORE YOU MOVE ON...

1. **Summarize** Reread page 25. What was Coyote Lady's new plan?

2. **Character's Point of View** Reread page 27. Why did Marco turn away when his father hid under the hood?

LOOK AHEAD Read pages 32–34 to find out how Marco feels when he reaches the United States.

Marco said nothing. He couldn't hear what Papá had said because of the noise in his ears, as if they were filled with cotton and bees. He felt as if he'd been molested, his body misappropriated. He pulled away from Papá's arm and climbed into the waiting van, this one with seats and windows. The door slid shut. Marco turned his face to the window and saw Coyote Lady and Flashlight Man driving away.

The others in the van smiled and talked as if they'd all just come from a party. The relief of **a successful crossing seemed to have unleashed their tongues**. Marco listened as they talked of their jobs in towns he'd never heard of before: Escondido, Solana Beach, Poway, Oceanside. Papá told them that he and his son were going to Encinitas to work in the flower fields and that it was his son's first time crossing over. Faces turned toward Marco.

Marco **cringed, his discomfort showing**. *Why did he have to mention me?*

One of the men laughed out loud. "At least you were not rolled inside a mattress like I was on my first time!"

"Or like me," said a young woman, grinning. "They dressed me as an *abuelita*, a grandmother, with a wig and

....

a successful crossing seemed to have unleashed their tongues making it to the United States made them talk a lot
cringed, his discomfort showing felt embarrassed

32

old clothes and had me walk across with another woman's identification. I was shaking the entire time."

Marco could only force a smile, but everyone else laughed.

Stories spilled from their lips about their first times or their friend's or family member's hiding inside hollowed-out bales of hay, cramped inside a hide-a-bed sofa from which the bed frame had been removed, buried in the middle of a truckload of crates filled with cackling chickens. Marco found himself chuckling and nodding **in co-misery**. An almost giddy air seemed to prevail as they all reveled in one another's bizarre stories and sometimes life-threatening circumstances.

He found himself eager to hear of each exploit and began feeling oddly proud and somehow connected to this unrelated group. **A strange camaraderie seemed to permeate the air**, and when one man told how he was hidden in a door panel of a truck, **smashed in a fetal position** for one hour, and thought he might suffocate, Marco laughed the hardest.

As the people were dropped off in towns along the way north, they shook hands with Marco and Papá and

....

in co-misery because he felt the same way

A strange camaraderie seemed to permeate the air He felt like the people in the van were his friends

smashed in a fetal position curled up like a baby

left them with the words *"Buena suerte,"* good luck. When Papá and Marco were the only ones left in the van and the driver finally headed up Freeway 5 toward Encinitas, Papá grinned at him. **"Okay now?"**

Marco nodded. "Okay." He looked out the window at the people in the cars on the freeway. They were all headed somewhere in the United States of America. Marco wondered how many were headed to a whole new world.

....

left them with the words said to them
Okay now? Do you feel better now?

BEFORE YOU MOVE ON...

1. **Character** At first, Marco was quiet and uncomfortable. How did he change after he heard the others' stories?

2. **Inference** Marco wondered if the travelers were "headed to a whole new world." What did this mean to Marco?

They Don't Mean It!
Lensey Namioka

Mary Yang's family is adjusting very well to American life, but Mary's friend Kim doesn't quite understand their responses.

They Don't Mean It!

Lensey Namioka

Our family moved here from China two years ago, and we thought we **were pretty well adjusted to American ways.** So my parents decided to give a party on Chinese New Year and invite some of our American friends.

When we first came to the United States, **we had a hard time getting used to** the different customs, but we gradually learned how things were done. We learned **American table manners**, for instance. We stopped slurping when we ate soup or ramen noodles. (At least we didn't slurp when we were with other Americans. When

....

were pretty well adjusted to American ways knew how Americans lived

we had a hard time getting used to it was difficult to learn

American table manners what Americans say and do when they eat together

we ate by ourselves at home, we still sneaked in a juicy slurp every now and then.)

Mother stopped complimenting people here on how old and fat they looked. She learned that Americans thought being old was **pitiful**, and that being slender was beautiful.

Father's English pronunciation was improving. He used to have trouble with the consonant *r*, so instead of "left" and "right," he would say "reft" and "light." Since he's a professional musician, making a correct sound is important to him, and he practiced until he mastered his *r*. Now he can tell me to pass him the Rice Krispies crisply.

I worked harder than anybody **at doing the right thing**, and I even kept a little notebook with a list of **English expressions** (one of my favorites was "It's raining cats and dogs"). I even **adopted** an American name: Mary. I knew my friends in school would have a hard time with my Chinese name, Yingmei, so now I'm Mary Yang.

I really believed that our family had adjusted completely. We had even joined in celebrating American holidays, such as Independence Day, Labor Day,

....

pitiful bad
at doing the right thing to act like an American
English expressions words and phrases used in the United States
adopted started using

Thanksgiving, Easter, Christmas, and New Year—
Western New Year, that is. My parents decided to show
our American friends what Chinese New Year was like.

Chinese New Year, which falls in late January or early
February, is sometimes called the Lunar New Year because
it's based on the phases of the moon. It doesn't always fall
on the same day in the solar calendar, but depends on
when the first new moon occurs after the winter solstice,
or the shortest day of the year. Anyway, in China it's also
called the Spring Festival, because by that time you're
pretty tired of winter and you're looking forward eagerly
to spring.

In China we celebrate the New Year by **setting off**
firecrackers, and we were delighted when we learned that
firecrackers were also set off here in Seattle's Chinatown at
New Year.

But eating special foods is the most important part
of the celebration. So a week before the party, we helped
Mother to shop and cook the special New Year dishes.
We had to serve fish, since the Chinese word for fish is
yu, which sounds the same as the word for "**surplus**." It's
good to have a surplus of money and other valuables.

Mother admitted that living in America for two years

....

setting off lighting
surplus extra

had **made her soft**, and she no longer felt like killing a fish with her own hands. These days, she bought dead fish, but she always apologized when she served it to our Chinese guests. When we first came to America, Mother used to keep live fish in the bathtub because that way she knew the fish would be fresh when it came time to cook it. Even for the New Year party, she bought a dead fish, but at least she went to a special store in Chinatown where they had live fish and killed it for you **on the spot**.

For our New Year dinner we also had to have noodles. We normally eat noodles on birthdays, because **the long strands stand for a long life**. Why noodles on New Year, then? Because in the old days, instead of having your own special birthday, everybody's birthday was on New Year's Day, no matter what day you were actually born on.

The New Year dish that involves the most work is the ten-vegetable salad. Mother tells us that each of the ten vegetables **is supposed to promote health**, and eating it on New Year makes you healthy for the whole year. I can understand why some of the vegetables are healthy—things like carrots, bean sprouts, and cabbage, which

....

made her soft changed her

on the spot at the store

the long strands stand for a long life they make you think of
a long, happy life

is supposed to promote health is very healthy

have lots of vitamins. But the salad also includes things like dried mushrooms and a kind of lichen. When I asked Mother why they were supposed to be healthy, she thought a bit and then admitted that she always included those ingredients because *her* mother and grandmother always included them.

So we got to work. We had to soak the dried ingredients. We had to wash the fresh vegetables and slice them up into thin strips. In addition to all the cooking, we vacuumed every room thoroughly, since we wanted to start the New Year with a really clean house. Mother said that we had to do the cleaning before New Year, because doing it on the day itself was bad luck. **It was believed that you'd sweep out good fortune together with the dirt.**

With all the cooking and the cleaning, I was **exhausted** by the time our guests arrived at our house for the New Year party.

The first of our guests to arrive were the Engs, a Chinese American family. Paul Eng, their son, was in Eldest Brother's class. Paul and Second Sister were beginning to be interested in each other, although we pretended we didn't notice. I was glad that Second Sister

....

It was believed that you'd sweep out good fortune together with the dirt. Many people thought that it was bad luck to sweep on New Year's Day.

exhausted very tired

had finally thrown away her Chinese cloth shoes. They had developed big holes, and we could see her toes wiggling around inside. Tonight she was wearing a new pair of sneakers she'd bought with her baby-sitting money.

The O'Mearas arrived next. Kim O'Meara was my best friend in school, and we'd been at each other's house lots of times. The last to arrive were the Conners. My youngest brother's best friend was Matthew Conner, who was a really good violinist and took lessons from my father.

"Happy New Year, Sprout!" Matthew said to Fourth Brother. "Sprout" was **my brother's nickname**, because for school lunch he used to eat sandwiches filled with stir-fried bean sprouts. Now he eats peanut butter and jelly sandwiches just like his friends, but the nickname stuck.

Because we had too many people to seat around the dining table, **we served dinner buffet style, and the guests helped themselves to the food**. When they saw all the dishes arranged on the dining table, they exclaimed at how beautiful everything looked.

"Oh, no, it's really plain, simple food," said Mother. "I've only added a few small things for the New Year."

....

my brother's nickname a name his friends called him

we served dinner buffet style, and the guests helped themselves to the food we put the food on a big table and people put food on their own plates

The guests **paid no attention** to her and began to help themselves. Mrs. Conner wanted to know how Mother had cooked the fish. Mrs. Eng said that she also cooked fish and served noodles on New Year, but she didn't do the ten-vegetable salad. Maybe it wasn't served in the part of China where her family originally came from.

Nobody had complaints about the food, from the way they devoured it and **came back for seconds**. The kids even ate up the salad. Kim O'Meara laughed when she saw her brother Jason taking a second **helping**. "Hey, Jason, I thought you hate vegetables!"

Jason's mouth was full, so he just mumbled an answer.

Mrs. O'Meara looked at me and smiled. "I bet you and your mom put a lot of work into making that salad, Mary. Doesn't it hurt to see it disappear **in a matter of minutes**?"

It *was* a lot of work to make the ten-vegetable salad. I got a blister on my finger from slicing all those celery and carrot sticks. "I'm glad to see how much you people like it," I said. "You'll all be very healthy this coming year!"

Looking at the platters of food getting emptied,

....

paid no attention did not listen
came back for seconds filled their plates again
helping plate of food
in a matter of minutes so quickly

I began to worry. "**We'd better do something about** dessert!" I whispered to Mother. At this rate, our guests would still be hungry after the main courses were finished.

"But I never make dessert!" Mother whispered back. Dessert isn't something Chinese normally eat at the end of a dinner.

So I ran into the kitchen, found a carton of almond cookies, and **hurriedly dumped** them on a platter. When I put the platter on the dining table, the cookies disappeared before I could say *abracadabra* (*abracadabra* was one of the words in my little notebook).

Since it was a weekday night, people didn't stay long after the last cookie crumb was eaten. **There was a congestion** at the front door as the guests thanked us for inviting them and showing them what a real Chinese New Year dinner was like.

"The fish was delicious!" Mrs. Eng said to Father. "I'll have to get the recipe from your wife **one of these days**. She's a wonderful cook, isn't she?"

"Oh, no, she's not a good cook at all," said Father.

....

We'd better do something about We should serve
hurriedly dumped quickly put
There was a congestion Everyone crowded together
one of these days soon

"You're just being polite."

I heard a little gasp from my friend Kim. She stared wide-eyed at Father.

"What's the matter, Kim?" I asked.

Instead of answering, Kim turned to look at Mrs. O'Meara, who was saying to my mother, "I *loved* your ten-vegetable salad. Even the kids loved it, and they don't usually eat their vegetables. You and the girls must have spent *hours* doing all that fine dicing and slicing!"

"The girls did the cutting, and I'm sorry they did such a terrible job," said Mother. "I'm embarrassed at how thick those pieces of celery were!"

I heard another little gasp from Kim, who was now staring at Mother. But I didn't get a chance to ask her what the problem was. The O'Mearas were going out the front door, and the rest of the guests followed.

* * *

"You're just being polite."
"You only said that she was a good cook to be nice."

BEFORE YOU MOVE ON...

1. **Conclusions** Reread pages 36–37 and find examples of how Mary's family tried to adjust to "American ways."

2. **Inference** Reread pages 43–44. What made Kim gasp? Why?

LOOK AHEAD Read pages 45–53 to find out why Kim says her mother's ham is terrible.

"How come your father and your mother were so nasty last night?" asked Kim when we were walking to the school bus stop the next morning.

"What do you mean?" I asked. I didn't remember Father or Mother acting nasty.

"It was when Mrs. Eng was telling your dad what a good cook your mom is," replied Kim.

That's right. Mrs. Eng did say something about Mother being a good cook. "So what's bothering you?" I asked.

Kim **stopped dead**. "Didn't you hear your dad?" she demanded. "He said that your mom wasn't a good cook at all, and that Mrs. Eng was just being polite!"

I still didn't understand why Kim was bothered. "So what? People are always saying things like that."

But Kim wasn't finished. "And then when my mom said how hard you worked to cut up the vegetables, your mom said she was embarrassed by what a terrible job you did in slicing!"

I had to laugh. "She doesn't mean it! It's just the way she talks."

When the school bus arrived and we got on, Kim began again. "Then why do your parents keep saying these

....

How come your father and your mother were so nasty Why were your parents so mean to each other

stopped dead stopped walking

bad things if they don't mean it? **I'd be really hurt** if my mom said I did a terrible job—after I worked so hard, too."

What Kim said made me thoughtful. I suddenly realized that whenever people said good things about us, my parents always **contradicted them** and said how bad we really were. We kids knew perfectly well that our parents didn't mean it, so **our feelings weren't hurt in the least**. It was just the way Chinese parents were supposed to talk.

Finally I said to Kim, "I think that if my parents agreed with the compliments, then that would be the same as bragging. It's good manners to contradict people when they **compliment** your children."

"It's bragging only if you say good things about *yourself*," protested Kim. "It's different when your parents are talking about *you*."

I shook my head. "We Chinese feel it's the same thing. Boasting about our children, or husband, or wife, is the same as boasting about ourselves. People even think it's bad luck."

....

I'd be really hurt I would feel terrible
contradicted them told them that they were wrong
our feelings weren't hurt in the least we did not feel bad
compliment say something nice about

It was Kim's turn to be thoughtful. "So that's why your parents never said what good musicians you were. That would be bragging, right?"

Music is the most important thing in our family. My elder brother plays the violin, my second sister plays the viola, and I play the cello. We all practice very hard, and I know Father thinks we are all doing well—only he has never said so to other people.

"The funny thing is," continued Kim, "your kid brother is the only one in your family who isn't a good musician. But I've never heard your parents say anything about how badly he plays."

I thought over what Kim said about Fourth Brother. He is the only one in our family who is no good at all with music. But we don't talk about **his terrible ear**. Finally I said, "It's like this: We're not hurt when we hear our parents say bad things about us, since we know they're only doing it because it's good manners. We know perfectly well that they don't mean it. But if they say my younger brother has a terrible ear, they'd really be telling the truth. So they don't say anything, because that would hurt his feelings."

Kim rolled her eyes. "Boy, this is confusing! Your parents can't tell the truth about your playing because

....

his terrible ear how badly he plays music

it would be bragging. And they can't say anything about your brother's playing because that would be telling the truth."

I grinned. "Right! You got it!"

I think Kim understood what I **was driving at**. She didn't make a face when she heard my mother saying that the cookies Second Sister baked for the PTA bake sale were terrible.

After our Spring Festival party, the days became longer, and cherry trees burst into bloom. The baseball season began, and Fourth Brother's team played an opening game against another school. My brother might have a terrible ear for music, but he was turning out to be a really good baseball player.

In the seventh inning Fourth Brother hit a home run, something he had wanted to do for a long time but **had never managed** before. All his teammates crowded around to **congratulate him**. "You did it, Sprout! You did it!" shouted Matthew Conner, his best friend.

Mr. Conner turned to Father. "I bet you're proud of the boy!"

....

was driving at tried to say
had never managed could not
congratulate him tell him what a good job he did

"He was just lucky when he hit that home run," said Father.

Overhearing the exchange, Kim turned to me and smiled. "**I see what you mean**," she whispered.

That Easter, the O'Mearas invited our family for dinner. I knew that Easter was a solemn religious holiday, but what I noticed most was that the stores were full of stuffed rabbits and fuzzy baby chicks. Chocolate eggs were everywhere.

For the dinner, Mrs. O'Meara cooked a huge ham. She had also made roast potatoes, vegetables, salad, and the biggest chocolate cake I had ever seen. I had eaten a lot at Thanksgiving dinners, but this time I **stuffed myself until I was bursting**. The rest of my family did pretty well, too. We all loved ham.

As Mrs. O'Meara started cutting up the cake for dessert, Mother said, "I'm not sure if I can eat one more bite. That was the best ham I've ever tasted!"

"Aw, that ham was terrible," said Kim. "I bet you could **do a lot better**, Mrs. Yang."

....

I see what you mean Now I understand what you were talking about

stuffed myself until I was bursting ate too much

do a lot better cook a better ham

There was a stunned silence around the table. Mrs. O'Meara stared at Kim, and her face slowly turned dark red.

I heard a low growl from Mr. O'Meara. "**You and I are going to have a little talk** later this evening, young lady," he said to Kim.

Our family **was speechless with surprise**. My parents, my brothers, and sister all stared at Kim. I was the most shocked, because Kim was my best friend, and in the two years since I've known her, I'd never seen her do or say anything mean. How could she say something so **cruel** about her own mother?

The rest of the evening was pretty uncomfortable. Our family left early, because we could all see that Mr. and Mrs. O'Meara were waiting impatiently to have their "little talk" with Kim as soon as we were gone.

Next morning at the school bus stop, Kim wouldn't even look at me. Finally I cleared my throat. "What made you talk like that to your mother, Kim?" I asked.

Kim whirled around. She looked furious. "B-but

....

You and I are going to have a little talk I want to talk to you about what you said

was speechless with surprise was so surprised that we did not know what to say

cruel mean

you were the one who t-told me that saying nice things about your own family was the s-same as bragging!" she stuttered. "Last night I was just trying **to act modest!**"

I finally saw the light. I saw how Kim had misunderstood what I had said. "Listen, Kim," I said, "Chinese *parents* are supposed to say critical things about their own *children*, and husbands and wives can say bad things about each other. But *young people* must **always be respectful to their *elders*.**"

The school bus came. "I guess I'll never understand the Chinese," sighed Kim as we sat down. At least we still sat together.

After school I went over to Kim's house and explained to Mrs. O'Meara about how the Chinese were supposed to sound modest about their own children. I told her that Kim had thought I meant children also had to sound modest about their parents. Mrs. O'Meara laughed. Although her laugh sounded a little forced, it was a good sign.

I soon forgot about Kim's **misunderstanding**, because

....

to act modest to show that I am not proud; to be humble

always be respectful to their *elders* never say anything bad about older family members

misunderstanding mistake

I had other things to worry about. Our school orchestra was giving its spring concert, and the conductor asked me to play a cello solo **as one of the numbers**. Father said I should play a dance movement from one of Bach's unaccompanied cello suites. It was a very hard piece, and I was really scared to play it in public. But Father said we should always try to meet challenges.

I practiced **like mad**. On the day of the concert, I was so nervous that I **was sitting on pins and needles** waiting for my turn to play ("sitting on pins and needles" was another expression in my little notebook). My legs were **wobbly** when it came time for me to walk to the front of the stage. But as I sat down with my cello and actually started playing, I **became so wrapped up in** the music that I forgot to be nervous.

After the concert, my friends came up to congratulate me. It was the proudest moment of my life. "You were great, Mary, simply great!" said Kim. Her eyes were shining.

Mother's eyes were shining, too. "Yes, she *was* good,"

....

as one of the numbers in the concert
like mad a lot
was sitting on pins and needles could not stay still
wobbly weak
became so wrapped up in was thinking so much about

she blurted out. Then she covered her mouth and looked embarrassed.

Kim turned to me and winked. "That's all right, Mrs. Yang. We all know **you didn't mean it**!"

....

you didn't mean it you did not want to say something nice

BEFORE YOU MOVE ON...

1. **Plot** Kim tried to be modest like Mr. and Mrs. Yang. Why didn't it work?

2. **Inference** On pages 52–53, Mrs. Yang complimented Mary, and Kim responded. What does this show about Mrs. Yang and Kim?

Lines of Scrimmage

Elsa Marston

Feeling like an outsider, Ameen has to find an inner strength he isn't sure he has.

Lines of Scrimmage
Elsa Marston

As he hurried up the walk to the adobe-style house that his family now called home, Ameen could hardly keep from leaping over the cactus garden. But it would **hardly do** for the new guy in the neighborhood to look like a fool, so he held back to the cool **gait** of an athlete. Inside, he felt as excited as a ten-year-old after his first trip on a roller coaster.

Almost too good to be true—Coach **starting him at quarterback**, in the very next game! Now he'd show them what he could do. Ameen Abu-Shakra, quarterback . . . leading one of the top high school teams in New Mexico!

....

hardly do not be good

gait walk

starting him at quarterback wanted him to be the quarterback in the beginning of the next football game

Just wait till he told **the folks**.

The front-door key stuck, which gave him time to **reflect on what had led up to this moment**. Even as a young kid in Detroit, **rooting** faithfully for the Lions, he'd wanted to play quarterback. In his eyes, a good QB was the ultimate American sports hero, the top man in that most American of all games, football. Not just because he had to be a great athlete—he also had to have brains, resourcefulness, courage. And above all, leadership. The quarterback was the man every eye focused on, the guy who held the team together and got them where they wanted to be. And now—through hard work and, admittedly, **a quirk of fate**—Ameen had almost reached that shining summit.

The key finally turned, and Ameen hustled inside. He was late. Practice had gone a bit longer than usual, and then Coach Martinez had held him for those few words that had **sent his spirits shooting to the skies**. The family would probably already have started to eat. His mom didn't like people straggling to the supper table, but he

....

the folks his parents

reflect on what had led up to this moment think about how he became the starting quarterback

rooting cheering

a quirk of fate luck

sent his spirits shooting to the skies made him so happy

hoped she'd forgive him quickly enough when she heard his news.

"Hey, I'm here! Just let me wash up and—"

"Yes, Ameen. Hurry up. Dinner's getting cold."

Her voice was flat, which tipped off Ameen before he slid into place in the small dining **alcove**. Even with a favorite meal on the table, garlic-marinated chicken and stuffed vine leaves, the emotional atmosphere felt heavy. His father was **in the midst of a tirade**, pausing hardly long enough to acknowledge Ameen's arrival.

Ameen groaned inwardly. He worried about his dad, **whose heart still yearned, without hope, for their home** back in Palestine. More than a dozen years earlier, when Ameen was only five, the family had left Ramallah for a better life in America, and now they'd just recently moved to Albuquerque to escape the frigid winters of Detroit. The dry climate seemed to help his dad's health, and his accounting business was doing well enough. But climate and income weren't enough to **bring peace of mind**.

Now, **touched off** by the evening news on television,

....

alcove room

in the midst of a tirade talking angrily

whose heart still yearned, without hope, for their home who missed their old home

bring peace of mind make him happy

touched off angered

Ameen's dad was venting his anger against the Israeli government and the U.S. Congress and the Palestinian leaders and everybody who made his people's lives so miserable. *Why does every dinner hour*, thought Ameen, *have to be like this?* But small wonder, when every day brought e-mail reports about the ongoing destruction of Palestinian homes and orchards and lives. Ameen felt the anger, too, but generally kept his mouth shut. No need to **add fuel to the fire**.

Finally Ameen's dad **wound** down, took a long swallow of soda, and lapsed into silence. Joumana, a couple of years younger than Ameen, was also quiet. She usually had plenty to say, with strong opinions on everything, but tonight she seemed **dispirited**.

In the moment's lull, Ameen saw his chance, hoping to **dispel** the heavy mood. "Hey, I'm starting at quarterback this week! What d'you think of that?"

It went over like a pile of wet towels. His mother looked up at him uneasily, brushing a curly strand of dark hair from her eyes.

....

add fuel to the fire make his dad angrier
wound calmed
dispirited bored
In the moment's lull While it was quiet
dispel end

"They want you to play quarterback, *habibi*? How can they? You're new here—they don't even know you."

Ameen let out a sigh of disappointment, then started to explain with exaggerated patience. "Okay, Mom, here's the deal. They're stuck. The first-string QB, the big hero Trent Worthing, the guy who put this team on the map last year, got caught cheating on a big exam. **He's on the bench**, maybe for the rest of the season. The second QB has a hamstring injury. That leaves me—'cause I came here with great recommendations from back in Detroit. So even though I'm an outsider, and new, and **an Arab**—and half of 'em probably think I'm a terrorist, God help me— Coach Martinez is giving me the chance."

"This is a bigger school," said his mother, frowning. "Maybe they play rougher here."

"Well, maybe they do. But I'm *good*, Mom. Come on! Don't you have faith in me?"

"Back home, in your old school, there were lots of Arabs. And Arabs on the team. You were **among your own kind**. They knew you and they'd protect you. But here, I don't know. Maybe it's different."

And maybe it would be different. Ever since the coach

He's on the bench He is not allowed to play football

an Arab from the Middle East

among your own kind with other people like you

had mentioned that Ameen might start at quarterback for a game or two, Ameen had lain awake at night thinking about it. Playing on this team, it had turned out, was not the way he'd expected. He'd supposed that in Albuquerque the people would be **pretty mixed** and he'd **fit in all right**, but the team members at his school were mostly big blond guys with all-American names and looks and attitudes. Of course there were a few Latinos, too, and a Navajo named Jeremy Yazzie, whom the guys respected for his fast feet but who didn't spend any more time in the locker room than he had to.

Then along came Ameen, with his olive skin and black hair and Arabic name. Even after two months of hard workouts with the team in late-summer heat, even after showing them what he could do, he still felt **as though he were walking on a knife edge**. That is, until this afternoon.

His mother ladled a spoonful of hummus onto his plate. "I'm afraid you'll get hurt, *habibi*," she said, her face **pinched with** worry. "Football's so violent. I hate all that violence—I've had all the violence I can stand. I wish

....

pretty mixed of different races
fit in all right be accepted
as though he were walking on a knife edge like he had to be careful
pinched with showing

you'd go out for track, or baseball. Or just concentrate on your studies, so you can get into a good college. I'm sure they can find somebody else."

"Mom . . . !" How **to get it across to her**? How to explain that this meant everything to him? To play quarterback for a team that the whole state was looking at—this was the chance of a lifetime! Sure, the all-American boys still thought of the position as *their* property . . . but now Ameen could show them that he was every bit as good and maybe better.

At last, while he was still **fumbling for words**, Joumana spoke up. "Mom, let him do it. He really wants to, and it's important, and you know he'll get into a good college anyway. He might even get a football scholarship."

"I can't help worrying," she answered. "Ever since nine-eleven, things have changed in this country. You read so much on the Internet . . . incidents, hate talk, discrimination, the government always making new rules. All of a sudden they're afraid of us. They hate us—and why?"

At last Ameen's dad roused himself. "I agree with

....

to get it across to her could he make her understand
fumbling for words trying to find something to convince his mom

your mother. Don't **make yourself conspicuous**."

"You people worry too much," Joumana said, her brown eyes now flashing, her fist clenched. "Sure, it's better to crawl around like an ant, if you want to avoid trouble—but you still may get stepped on. What do you think it's like for me at that school? I know people whisper behind my back. But not everybody. I have friends—not just Arab girls—and they accept me like I am."

Glad to see some of her usual spunk, Ameen still couldn't pass up a chance to tease her a little. "You'd have it easier, Jou-jou, if you didn't wear the headscarf. Mom doesn't."

Now Joumana focused her fire on Ameen. "That's her choice, and this is mine. It's part of who I am. It's a statement. I am a Muslim, I am an Arab, and I'm proud of it!"

"Well, if you want to stick out—"

"So? What's the difference? I've got the guts to stick out and be myself in the hallways, and you've the guts to stick out and show them on the football field." Joumana turned to glare at her parents. "And we shouldn't **stand in his way**, Mom and Baba."

....

make yourself conspicuous let people notice that you are different

stand in his way stop him from doing what he wants to do

Way to go, girl, thought Ameen. *I'll remember that.*

He reached for another skewer of broiled chicken; he really had to put on some more weight. He wished his dad would eat more—and **sound off** less.

....

sound off talk

BEFORE YOU MOVE ON...

1. **Conflict** Reread pages 57 and 60. Why did Ameen feel both excited and worried about starting the game as quarterback?

2. **Comparisons** Why did Ameen's father say, "Don't make yourself conspicuous"? How was this different from what Joumana said?

LOOK AHEAD Read pages 65–76 to see what happens in Ameen's first game as quarterback.

A few nights later, showered and deodorized, his thick hair still wet, Ameen headed for the locker room door. He'd taken some knocks in the game, but overall he felt about eight feet tall. It had all gone so well, he could hardly believe it, **a dream scenario**. The guy with the hamstring pull had managed to play a little, but Coach Martinez had put in Ameen for most of the game. And he'd done it. **He'd marched those guys to a good win against a tough team, a real upset.**

Just outside the locker room, a crowd confronted him—lots more people than he'd been expecting. Reporters started shooting questions.

"Your first game at quarterback, right, son?"

"You're new this year, aren't you? From Detroit?"

"How'd it feel when you saw Yazzie get his hands on that great touchdown pass?"

"Think your team will make it to state championship again this year?"

Ameen stammered his way through the first few questions, then relaxed and took them more in stride.

....

a dream scenario it was perfect

He'd marched those guys to a good win against a tough team, a real upset. He helped the team win even when no one expected their team to win.

This was a QB's bonus, this rush of acclaim. **He was the man of the hour, spokesman for the whole team.** The price of fame! Well, he'd pay that price—and gladly. Of course the sportswriters and TV reporters wanted a few good quotes, so he'd have to think fast. And be careful. **Give the team all the credit**: *Hey, we work together. I just got off a couple of good passes—all those other guys made it happen. Great team, great coach. You bet we're headed for the championship—just watch us.*

As Ameen thought back over the game, however, he began to recall some specific moments. Sure, he'd done fine. His arm had been strong and quick, he'd moved well, and he'd made a couple of good option plays. He could almost still hear the crowd roar with excitement. But he'd heard something else, too, that he must have tried to forget. Now it came back to him . . . the **trash talk**. Not the usual stuff you expect in the heat of battle, but ethnic insults, slurs aimed at his heart.

It started in the second half, when the score was tied. They'd timed it just as he was trying to call out the plays,

....

He was the man of the hour, spokesman for the whole team. He was the most important person; everyone listened to what he said.

Give the team all the credit Say that everyone played well

got off a couple of good passes threw the ball well a couple of times

trash talk insults; mean things the other team said to him

and every time he got knocked down. He couldn't see which guys were doing it—maybe most of them, maybe just a couple. But one thing he was aware of: his own linemen had kept quiet. They'd done their job protecting him, but they'd said nothing to shut up that kind of trash talk.

For a while he'd **let it get to him**. He'd **blown a couple of plays**, and his team had lost control of the ball. On the sidelines he'd felt anger, fury against the unfairness and stupid hatred. Then, back on the field, something else had kicked in—a big spurt of energy. From his anger? Yes, anger seemed to be **fueling his strength and clearing his head** at the same time. *Okay, call me anything you like— it'll just make me tougher!*

And things had changed. He'd called the plays more firmly, moved faster, thrown with greater authority. Then that faked handoff that the opponents couldn't read, allowing a quick pass to the tight end—and a touchdown. And a little later, that high, long, beautiful pass to Jeremy Yazzie. Yes, he'd shown them what he could do **under fire**.

··

let it get to him felt bad about what they said

blown a couple of plays made mistakes

fueling his strength and clearing his head making him stronger and be able to think better

under fire when he was feeling stress

Of course he didn't say anything about that to the reporters. Nope, the other guys had given them a good game, and his team had come through just great. Next Friday night's game would be even better.

After the reporters dispersed, Ameen left the building and headed for the parking lot, his face warm with excitement. He could hardly wait to tell his folks. They didn't share his interest in the game—and more to the point, they didn't feel comfortable sitting in the stands. But they'd be proud; they'd be glad for him.

* * *

Two weeks later, Ameen sat in the locker room, elbows on knees, towel over his head. It was late and most of the players had already left. Ameen was in no hurry to go. If there was anybody still hanging around out there, let 'em talk to somebody else. **Eight sacks in one game— crushing ones.** What could he say if anybody asked him how that had happened? *Just didn't move fast enough, too panicked to see an open receiver . . . choked before I could get rid of the ball?*

Eight sacks in one game—crushing ones. The other team stopped him eight times in one game.

Time after time he'd been **blitzed**, those defensive linemen just raring to tear his head off. And they'd nearly succeeded. He could still **see them in his mind's eye**, barreling right past his guards, grabbing him, hurling him to the ground, falling on him hard—two, three, four of them. Even the memory made him ache.

Last week there had been three sacks, and he'd limped for days with a kicked ankle and bruised ribs. His team had won the game, but just barely. Tonight they'd lost by three touchdowns. Ameen could imagine the write-ups in the morning's paper: *Does this team really have a chance with newcomer Ameen Abu-Shakra still **shakily subbing for** Trent Worthing, who led the team so sensationally last year?*

Under his towel, Ameen became conscious of voices. A couple of guys were still in the locker room, and he recognized the voice of one of the linemen.

"Think Martinez will put Trent back in before it's too late?"

"He's got to. He has *got* to. We can't go on like this."

"Man, we need Trent. He's our only hope."

"My dad'll talk to Coach. And the athletics director—

....

blitzed tackled; knocked down
see them in his mind's eye remember
shakily subbing for not doing a good job in place of

they're tight. Don't worry, we'll get him back. There's a two-week break. A lot can happen in that time."

The voices **trailed off**, and the sound of footsteps ended with the clang of the locker-room door. Ameen knew the conversation had been intended to **get under his skin**; if it hadn't already been crystal clear to him why he'd been sacked so many times, it was now. With that great game two weeks earlier, he'd become a threat to the power structure. Some of his teammates, it seemed, were willing to **risk throwing the game, just to force him out of the QB position** and get their buddy back in there.

For a minute the room was quiet. Then Ameen became conscious of another presence. The wooden bench wobbled as someone sat down beside him.

"Hey, I know you're in there, Abu-Shakra. Come out of your tent."

Jeremy Yazzie. What did he want? Ameen **was in no mood for a chat**, especially with a guy he didn't know how to talk to.

----

trailed off stopped

get under his skin make him feel bad

risk throwing the game, just to force him out of the QB position lose the game so that he would not be able to play quarterback again

was in no mood for a chat didn't want to talk

"I'm cool," he muttered. "Just want to sit here a little longer."

"Let's see it. Your face, man."

Something about the voice, low but compelling, made Ameen pull back the towel and sit up a little straighter. Jeremy whistled.

"Oh, your mom's not going to like that. They really let you have it, didn't they?"

Ameen hadn't looked at himself in the mirror after his shower, but he could imagine he wasn't very pretty. The **abrasions stung**, and one eye throbbed. Must've been the time someone knocked his helmet off and his face got ground into the **turf**.

"Yup," Jeremy repeated softly, "the white boys let you have it all right. But you can't really blame 'em. They just wanted to get something across to you. For your own good, man."

Ameen glanced at him, scowling. "My own good?"

"Teach you your place."

What was this Indian guy trying to do? Uneasy, Ameen turned away. He'd heard that Indians could be

....

abrasions stung cut and wounds hurt

turf field

"Teach you your place." "They wanted to show that a Palestinian is not good enough to be quarterback."

prickly. He'd never seen any Indians in Detroit, didn't know much about them. Jeremy looked like a regular guy and he could play, all right, but Ameen was never quite sure how to read that calm, unrevealing expression. Anyway, he was in no hurry to know Indians any better.

"We've got something in common, you and me," said Jeremy.

"Sure. We both got black hair."

"Not what I mean. Listen." Jeremy spoke in an undertone. "It's like we've both gotten sacked—because **we're both up against the white boys' club, the ones God meant to have everything**. My people were here first, and we ended up on reservations. You came from a refugee camp or something. Both our folks had to **give way** when the white folks wanted what we'd got."

Ameen bristled. For one thing, he was as white as any of those other guys, and he didn't like Jeremy making it sound like he wasn't. Just not blond and blue-eyed. But as he thought it over, he understood. In the same way the Indians had had to yield, his people had been expected to

....

we're both up against the white boys' club, the ones God meant to have everything the white boys try to stop us because they think they are better than Arabs and Native Americans

give way lose something they had

hand over Palestine to someone "more worthy."

"So?" he muttered, getting up to wet the towel at a sink and place it against his bruised cheek. "Do we roll over and play dead?"

Jeremy gave a short laugh. "Nope, there's another way." He became serious again. "Look, man. We've got a two-week break and then the two biggest games of the season. You're gonna play. You're gonna quarterback. Because you're good, man. **You're gonna get yourself fixed up and fired up and get back in there.**"

"No way." Ameen shook his head and sat down on the bench. He had another painful flash of memory—those defensive linemen coming right for him, nobody stopping them. Once again he felt like an animal transfixed by the predator's glare. "I can't go through what I did today. They'll just pull the same thing, and I'll get killed. I mean really killed. I can't take it anymore."

Jeremy grimaced. "Yeah, I know. It was dirty. But I don't want . . ." He paused uncertainly for a moment. "I

---

hand over Palestine to someone "more worthy" give their land to someone else

You're gonna get yourself fixed up and fired up and get back in there. You are going to get ready to play again.

don't want you to go down. You **showed your stuff when you got half a chance**, and you can do it again. You can rub *their* faces in the dirt."

"No way. **I've had enough.** Look, Yazzie . . . I hate to say it, but I'm scared."

"And you sounded it. Calling off the plays, you sounded it—and the battle was half lost then. But that was today. The next two games are gonna be different."

"You got a plan?" Ameen let his voice sound as bitter as he felt.

There was no glint of humor in Jeremy's eyes as he faced Ameen. "First of all, you and I are gonna put in extra time. After practice every day, we're gonna pass and receive and run until we can do it **blindfolded**. Until you can **hit me** in the next county—or swimming across the Rio Grande."

"You're crazy. If I came home any later and more beat, my **folks'd have fits**." Even as he said it, though, Ameen thought, *Yes, they would . . . but Joumana would stand up for me. All the way.*

....

showed your stuff when you got half a chance showed that you were good in the first game

I've had enough. I quit; I cannot do this anymore.

blindfolded without seeing

hit me throw the ball to me

folks'd have fits parents would be very angry

"They'll get used to it," Jeremy went on more easily. "And that's not all. I'm taking you someplace like nowhere you've ever been before, and you're gonna surprise yourself."

"Yeah? Where's this place? What am I going to do?"

"A canyon in Arizona where my aunts live—it's called Canyon de Chelly. You're gonna conquer the canyon—and then make your peace with it. And you'll be a different guy when you come out."

He spoke so lightly, Ameen took it as a joke. But it was a joke **so far from his comprehension that he didn't know how to respond**. He stalled for a moment, getting up again to head for his locker. Then he said, "Sure. Coach'll love for us to go to some canyon next weekend. Yazzie, you are really **nuts**."

A couple of days later, Jeremy stopped Ameen in the **corridor** between classes. "Hey, I talked to Coach about us going to the canyon. He was kinda surprised—we're supposed to keep close to home on no-game weekends, in case he calls an extra practice. But you know, Coach likes

---

so far from his comprehension that he didn't know how to respond he could not understand and he did not know what to say

nuts crazy, strange

corridor hall

to make an unexpected decision now and then. He got to thinking about it—and he said yes."

"You're kidding. He doesn't mind if we go to a canyon in Arizona?" Ameen shook his head in disbelief. "Man, that's too far out. A long drive—and for what? Just a change in scenery? It won't work."

"Trust me," said Jeremy, tapping his forehead like a **sage**. "I know."

....

sage wise person

BEFORE YOU MOVE ON...

1. **Comparisons** How did Ameen play in the first game? What happened two weeks later? Why did things change?

2. **Paraphrase** Reread pages 71–72. Tell in your own words why Ameen doesn't trust Jeremy.

LOOK AHEAD Read pages 77–84 to find out what Jeremy and Ameen do at the canyon.

In any case, their own extra hours of practice came first. As they worked together hour after sweaty hour, Ameen began to revise his ideas about Jeremy, seeing him more as a person, not just a receiver. And the experience intrigued him. Growing up in Detroit, he reflected, he'd never really known many people outside the Arab community. He felt as though a window was opening for him, offering him an interesting new view. Finally, Ameen agreed to **go along with Jeremy and his crazy notion**.

On Thursday evening, he approached the family dining table **with the weight of uncertainty on his shoulders**. The scene started out exactly as he'd expected.

"What?" Ameen's father sat up straight. "That Indian kid wants to take you to a desert somewhere? **Not on your life.**"

"A canyon, Baba, not a desert. There are trees. It's a famous place."

"If it's that nice," said his mother diplomatically, "maybe we can all go there someday. But you can't go alone, Ameen. God knows what might happen to you."

....

go along with Jeremy and his crazy notion do what Jeremy wanted

with the weight of uncertainty on his shoulders feeling nervous

Not on your life. I will not let you go.

Joumana had been staring at her brother, open-mouthed. Now she shrieked, "Oh, you lucky! I've heard of Canyon de Chelly—it's beautiful. And you'll be staying with a Navajo family? Oh, you are so *lucky!*"

"Canyons are dangerous," their mother said worriedly.

"There's nothing bad, Mom—Jeremy told me. No wild animals, no tornadoes, blizzards, floods, avalanches. Nothing that could hurt anybody. Just goats and apple trees. That's what they grow there."

"**It's the chance of a lifetime for him**, Mom and Baba," argued Joumana. "He'll learn something besides football—geology, ancient history, good stuff. You don't want him to be a dumb **jock** all his life, do you?"

The question passed unanswered, and a short lull set in. Then Ameen's mother came up with another thought. "But what would you do, *habibi*? How would you pass your time?"

Ah, thought Ameen, a practical question. That's a good sign. "I don't know, Mom, just hang out. Take it easy, maybe help on the farm a little. Chop wood."

"You, a city boy?" said Ameen's father.

"Of course he can chop wood! He can pick apples and

....

It's the chance of a lifetime for him He might never be able to do this again

jock athlete

feed the goats," Joumana put in. "Let him go, Baba! Mom, make Baba let him go."

The more Joumana worked on her parents and raved about her brother's good fortune, the more interested Ameen got. Maybe he was, in fact, lucky. He **ratcheted up his own arguments**. And finally his folks **gave in**, although with worry lines in their foreheads and caution-heavy voices. Ameen was surprised that victory had come so easily. Maybe living in the open spaces of the Southwest was loosening them all up a bit.

"Well, anyway," said his mother with a sigh, "you must take it easy, dear. Get a good rest. You've been practicing much too hard lately. Don't do anything dangerous. I'll make some *baklawa* for you to take to those people."

"Right, Mom. Thanks, folks, thanks a lot." Ameen gave his sister a wink, as if to say *I owe you, Jou-jou.* ***You can count on me someday.***

And here he was at the canyon, gazing in amazement at cliffs glowing pink in the last rays of the setting sun. The jolting drive in Jeremy's dilapidated old blue pickup had

....

ratcheted up his own arguments worked hard to make them understand his ideas

gave in agreed to let him go

You can count on me someday. *I will do something good for you in the future.*

almost been adventure enough for Ameen. But then came the long hike down a trail overlooking awesome cliffsides and wind-sculpted rock towers, then more miles to slog through the soft sand of the canyon bottom to reach the farm, and an embarrassing struggle to set up a borrowed tent under spreading cottonwood trees—with three curious horses **close at hand**, watching every move.

Jeremy's aunt, wearing a heavy turquoise brooch on her denim shirt, had welcomed him quietly with a gentle warmth. After a hot supper in the open-sided shade house, Ameen was glad enough to say good night early and head off for his tent under the star-filled skies. **He had no inkling what the next day would bring.**

Now it was Saturday noon. Prodded by Jeremy, Ameen had just climbed *out* of the canyon. Hardly realizing he'd reached the top and was on level ground at last, he stared around him. An exposed layer of limestone stretched invitingly across the plateau, like a lumpy quilt thrown hastily over a bed. Exhausted, he lowered himself to the bare stone.

"I can't believe I just did that," he said flatly. "I cannot *believe* it."

....

close at hand near them

He had no inkling what the next day would bring. He did not know what would happen tomorrow.

"Well, man, you did. Don't you feel good?" Jeremy sat down near him and grinned, **not a hint of strain in his broad face**.

"Why did I ever let you talk me into this?" Ameen was still breathing hard, from both exertion and fear. "This is the craziest thing I've ever done. I'm a city boy—**I know the *streets*!** I can't climb up a canyon wall, like a lizard."

Jeremy shrugged. "But you made it. My aunts and cousins can do it in the dark. Navajos think those iron handrails are just for wimps. Now, I must admit, I touched one a couple of times, but—"

"Yazzie, without those rails, **you'd be mopping me up off** the canyon floor right now."

"Nah, I wouldn't like that. But I knew you wouldn't fall. The whole point is for you to know it, too."

Ameen shut his eyes to the spectacular views at the canyon rim, the twisted formations of buff-colored slickrock, the spindly pines tucked into crevices, the rust-stained cliffs rising sheer on the far side, the brilliant blue of the cloudless Arizona sky. He'd appreciate all that later. Right now he was reliving the climb, in his imagination again clambering up those impossibly steep walls of wind-

....

not a hint of strain in his broad face not looking tired at all
I know the *streets*! I'm not used to the canyons!
you'd be mopping me up off I'd be down there on

eroded rock, **feeling for the little indentations** Jeremy said had been carved by the Ancient Ones a thousand years earlier. Whenever they'd reached a resting spot, he'd nearly collapsed, gasping for breath—but not for long, before Jeremy pressed him to push on and up the next nearly vertical rock face.

The late October sun was high but not too hot, and the breeze was light. Still, Ameen felt **clammy** inside his sweatshirt. The sweat of fear and panic. He'd thought he knew all about that feeling, after those last games when the defensive line had come after him . . . but this kind of fear was something else—**the awareness that one unsure step, one stumble, could be fatal**. Meanwhile, he noticed with a twinge of resentment, Jeremy had stretched out and was already peacefully snoozing. **Did anything rattle the guy?**

When Ameen had fully caught his breath and felt his heartbeat more or less back where it should be, he nudged Jeremy. **"Now what, chief?"**

....

feeling for the little indentations trying to find the places to put his hands and feet that

clammy wet and cold

the awareness that one unsure step, one stumble, could be fatal knowing that if he made a mistake, he could die

Did anything rattle the guy? Was he afraid of anything?

"Now what, chief?" "What should we do now?"

Lazily, Jeremy pulled himself halfway up, then jumped to his feet. "We go down. I'm hungry, man. She promised us fry bread . . . if we came back."

"Down . . . like the same way we came up?"

Jeremy gestured toward a view farther along the rim, where the cliff rose nearly a thousand feet straight up from the canyon floor. "We could go that way—it'd be quicker. But **on second thought** . . ."

No, the **circuitous** path by which they'd climbed up the slickrock was obviously the better choice. Ameen stood and stamped the stiffness out of his legs. Reluctantly, he followed Jeremy to the edge of the plateau, where the limestone dropped off and countless thin layers of compressed sand had, in eons past, created the contours and bulges of slickrock below.

"Hey," he said, "I always heard that when you're in high places, you're supposed to never look down. How can I *not* look down?"

"You have to," Jeremy answered **nonchalantly**. "The point is, down's just one part of **the whole picture**, no worse than any other part. Don't think of it as your

----

on second thought when I think about it again
circuitous winding
nonchalantly casually
the whole picture what you see

enemy. Trust your boots—they're not afraid of down—and take another step. How's that for comforting advice?"

"God help me," muttered Ameen, starting to sidestep down the steep incline.

"Sure, get Allah to give you a hand."

The good-natured jibe irritated Ameen. A few times during the past week, he and Jeremy had **tossed around quips about their respective religions**, but Ameen wasn't going to take the bait this time. He'd need every bit of his self-control to reach the bottom in one piece. He still couldn't imagine why he'd **let himself be talked into this crazy adventure**. And just because, he thought as he turned to face the rock and started to back awkwardly down, **groping** with his boot for a secure foothold, just because he'd wanted to show the world what a great quarterback he could be.

* * *

....

tossed around quips about their respective religions joked about each other's religious beliefs

let himself be talked into this crazy adventure agreed to come with Jeremy

groping searching, feeling

BEFORE YOU MOVE ON...

1. **Sequence** What did Ameen and Jeremy do on Saturday? How did Ameen feel about the experience?

2. **Inference** What did Jeremy want to teach Ameen? How might that help Ameen?

LOOK AHEAD Read pages 85–90 to find out if the canyon trip helps Ameen on the football field.

Now, back in the security of his school's football stadium, Ameen watched the last game of the season, against the strongest opponent the team had faced yet. Helmet in hand, he sat on the bench.

At least Jeremy was in the action—he'd caught a couple of Trent Worthing's sensational passes. Yes, clearly something had happened during those two weeks between games, and it was generally agreed that Trent Worthing **had paid his debt to society**. He'd won the game last week. The second-string QB had played for a while, and Ameen, too, had gotten in a few plays. But it had been the star quarterback's win. Half the female population of the school, by Ameen's **conservative estimate**, had blitzed Trent Worthing after the game.

Play had stopped. There was a long time-out while players and referees discussed a penalty. As he sat on the bench, Ameen was aware that he did not feel as agitated as he might have. Something had **sunk into** him during those two days in the canyon, and he felt different in a way he could not quite identify. Now, during the break in action, he **allowed his thoughts to wander back to** the

....

had paid his debt to society had been punished enough

conservative estimate guess

sunk into changed

allowed his thoughts to wander back to remembered; thought again about

brilliant Arizona sky and the towering rock walls.

The first climb to the top had scared him half to death. And the second climb, up a treacherously jumbled rock slide, had been only a little less **daunting**. But halfway along the third trail, finding himself hundreds of feet above the canyon floor and still alive, Ameen felt a different emotion start to take over. *He was doing it, something he'd never even imagined before, he was doing it! Aware of danger but focusing on the step ahead of him, knowing he had the power to take that step, and the one after that.* Yes, as Jeremy had promised, Ameen was surprising himself. Maybe those Navajo guys **were on to something**.

The feeling of **elation** had stayed with Ameen after his return. He'd worked even harder at practice. When he called out plays in scrimmage, his voice **had a strong ring**. His passes hit Jeremy and the other receivers consistently. Coach Martinez had good words for him. Hope was budding again.

But now, in the last matchup of the season, there he was—still on the bench.

....

daunting difficult and scary
were on to something knew something important
elation happiness
had a strong ring was strong and clear

Near the end of the third quarter, Ameen began to grow restless. He could feel the cold hand of doubt and resentment start to squeeze his heart. *Come on, give me a chance! It's only fair. But who ever said the world is fair? Who can help me? No, I'm alone. Like my dad says, Palestinians alone against the world.*

The sudden thud of clashing bodies and shoulder pads on the field **jarred his thoughts**. *Violence.* His mom had called football violent . . . and the word reminded him of common phrases from the American media. "Palestinian violence," "Palestinian terrorism," "Palestinians, violent people."

He tried to suppress those thoughts. After all, Jeremy was on his side. Jeremy, too, knew what it was like to feel alone. But Ameen couldn't **quite pry the cold fingers of resentment off his heart**.

His team was **trailing by four points**. Only three minutes left in the game. Ameen's focus sharpened, then grew intense. There seemed to be an injury on the field. Yes, Trent Worthing was coming off! Held up by a trainer, he was hopping on one foot.

An instant later, Ameen saw Coach Martinez beckon

....

jarred his thoughts made him look at the field

quite pry the cold fingers of resentment off his heart stop feeling resentful, or angry that things weren't fair

trailing by four points losing by four points

to him. "You're in, Abu-Shakra."

Snapping on his helmet, Ameen ran onto the field. What did that mean, putting in the outsider at the critical moment? Was he up to the pressure? Would **the line hold**—or let him down again? He hoped at least his anger would drive him, the way it had before.

As he reached the huddle, however, Ameen realized that the anger had already faded. A different feeling was growing in him, rising from a depth that he was just starting to know. *Do what you have to do. Look at those faces around you like you're as sure of them as solid rock.*

He faced the team. "We've got three minutes. We can **turn this thing around**. We can do it—we *will* do it. Okay, here's the play . . ."

*Trust your boots. Look down, but don't **dread** it. When you **take the snap**, let your feet carry you out of harm's way. See what you need to see . . . the next step . . . Jeremy in midfield. You're not at the mercy of a hostile world. Things'll be flying, but you're in control. . . .*

The clock moved on, while the team struggled for every gain. With only seconds remaining, they made it

....

the line hold his teammates protect him
turn this thing around start to win the game
dread fear
take the snap get the ball

to the twenty-yard line. Coach **sent in the play**, a daring one that could make or lose the game. Ameen called it in the huddle.

But when they took position at the line of scrimmage, Ameen caught his breath in panic. The opposing players had shifted. Somehow, whether by a calculated risk or a lucky guess, they'd lined up in a way that would wipe out any chance for the play to work.

He'd never called an audible—made a last-second change on his own, right at the line of scrimmage. But he'd have to now, **or they hadn't a hope**. No more than a few seconds left. He called out new signals, and the play started.

With the ball in hand, he backed up and looked for his receiver. Jeremy was swamped, guys all over him. The tight end? No, he was covered, too. Then, to his amazement, Ameen saw **a hole start to open**. Could he make it? He shouted. A couple of his guards turned and saw him point. Almost instantly they hurled themselves at the attackers, bulldozing players out of the way. Ameen shot through. For twenty yards he zigzagged, eluding some hands, ripping through others—only to be grabbed on

....

sent in the play told them the plan
or they hadn't a hope or they would lose the game
a hole start to open a place where he could run

the two-yard line. But he kept his feet going, scrambling, driving for every inch . . . and **by the time he was finally brought down, he had made it into the end zone**.

Ameen's job was over. Dimly aware of the uproar, he disentangled himself from the pile of tacklers, got up, and headed for the bench. An instant later, his teammates were upon him. Someone whacked him on the helmet, the thump of celebration, and then several more. Someone punched him in the arm, the punch of approval, and others just chanted his name. "A-boo-sha-kra, A-boo-sha-kra!"

Maybe the reporters and fans would **give him a rush**, and maybe not. Either way, it'd be cool. What mattered more to Ameen than another burst of fame and glory was that he, the outsider, had won his own game. Then, as he saw Jeremy come leaping toward him, Ameen seemed to hear the echo of his friend's voice: words he'd remember all his life.

*Don't **focus on** the danger, man. Just take the next step.*

---

by the time he was finally brought down, he had made it into the end zone when he stopped, he had already reached the goal

give him a rush come talk to him

focus on think about

BEFORE YOU MOVE ON...

1. **Cause and Effect** How did the trip to the canyon affect Ameen?

2. **Inference** Reread page 90. How did Ameen win "his own game"? Why was this more important than "another burst of fame and glory"?

The Green Armchair

Minfong Ho

Sopeap envies Thomas's connection to his grandfather—until she realizes the value of her own heritage.

The Green Armchair
Minfong Ho

That it was heavy she **could tell** immediately from the way it was being dragged across the bed of the pickup truck, the thick canvas around it scraping against the metal as it moved. But that it was also valuable she **surmised** only a moment later, when the young man pushed his shoulder against it, then stopped. With one good shove, he might have pushed it right over the side of the truck, but no—he **dismissed this option** with an impatient toss of his head and instead jumped off the truck.

The young man strode across the pavement so quickly that Sopeap didn't have time to **click off** the city-building

....

could tell knew
surmised knew
dismissed this option changed his mind
click off turn off

computer game she had been playing. As he opened the storefront door, a rush of cold air blew in with him, swirling eddies of sawdust and wood chips around in the big room.

"Hi, could you **give me a hand** with that thing?" he called. His voice, like the gust of fresh air, was so vibrant it startled her.

She stared at him. *Thomas*, she thought. It was the boy who sat three rows in front of her in algebra class, next to the window, the morning sun catching the glints from his blazing red curls, so that his head looked like it was on fire. *Thomas Ramsey*. For an awful moment she thought she had said his name out loud, but then realized **it had only been in her mind**.

Sopeap forced a smile. "Sure," she said, pleasantly surprised by how casual, how American, she sounded. "Be right with you."

"Hey, aren't you in my history class?" he asked.

"Algebra," she said quietly. At least he recognized her. She had long since noticed him, **intrigued by the aloof, easy banter he carried on** with his classmates, as if he were looking at them from the wrong end of a telescope.

....

give me a hand help me
it had only been in her mind she had only thought his name
intrigued by the aloof, easy banter he carried on interested in the confident way he spoke and acted

A bit of a loner, and liking it that way. *Sort of like me*, she had sometimes thought, clutching onto her solitude as tightly as she held her textbooks, as she walked behind him after class.

"Algebra, history, whatever," he said, laughing. "What's that?" Another long stride, and he was next to her, peering into the computer monitor.

Phnom Penh, she said silently, wondering if he would even know that that was the name of the city where she had grown up, **been forced to evacuate**, and left behind forever. A fantasy Phnom Penh, of course, but she had drawn in the main roads of the city as she had remembered them, and the river running through it.

"Hey cool," he said. "You put ballparks in the industrial zone!"

Something the Communist regime in Cambodia would never have done, Sopeap thought, but she wasn't sure she could say it **glibly** enough, so she just kept quiet.

"Did you use any cheats?"

"Never," Sopeap said. "And it's not a pirated copy, either."

....

A bit of a loner, and liking it that way. He liked to be alone.
Sort of like me *He is like me*
been forced to evacuate been told to leave
glibly easily

Tom laughed. "Hey, **no offense**," he said. "I'm not much good at the game, so I use cheats when I can. Any chance you could burn me a copy of the CD?"

Sopeap hesitated. "I could try, but . . . but it's probably protected by . . . you know . . . "

"Sure . . . **copyrights**. They're getting so uptight about that." He leaned on the table and peered into her monitor. "How big is your city?" he asked.

Instinctively, she drew away and got up. Too close too quickly, he had **invaded** the invisible bubble that protected her, that not even her own family would have **intruded** into.

"What was it you wanted help with?" she asked, nodding at the pickup truck outside the door.

"Oh yeah, right." He led the way out to the sidewalk, while she quickly saved her game and minimized it on the monitor.

Once outside, Sopeap realized that it would take patience rather than just brute strength to move that huge bundle off the truck. Thomas **was adamant that it be handled** very carefully, even delicately. "Don't drop it,"

....

no offense I didn't want to insult you

copyrights laws that don't allow making copies

invaded entered

intruded come

was adamant that it be handled told her that they should lift it he said. **"It's fragile."**

Carefully she helped nudge it onto Tom's shoulders, **steadying** it as he slowly set it down onto the sidewalk.

"What is it?" she asked.

"An armchair," he said.

Arm-chair, she repeated silently. Did that mean a chair for an arm, or a chair made of arms, or maybe a chair with four legs that were shaped like arms?

She held open the heavy glass door as he pushed the bulky thing through. The words SADOWSKY'S FURNITURE REPAIR were still painted on it in **ornate** black lettering, even though Sopeap's father had said many times that he intended to replace it with THE GREAT ANGKOR REPAIR CENTER.

It wasn't until they had **wrestled the bundle** to the middle of the room and peeled the canvas sheet from it that Sopeap saw what an armchair was. "Arm," she said, touching one of the wooden armrests on it. "Arm-chair." Of course, it was a chair with arms.

Old but sturdy, it had obviously been used for a long time. The leather was cracked and worn thin in places.

The brass tacks holding the leather in place were

....

"It's fragile." "It can break easily."

steadying holding

ornate fancy

wrestled the bundle brought the package

rusty, and its wooden legs were chipped. But the wooden structure of the chair itself was still solid.

"It belonged to my granddad," Tom said. "He'd sit in it every night reading the newspaper, for as long as I can remember."

"You want it . . . **redone**?" Sopeap asked. "For him?"

"Yeah . . . but not for him. He died last year." He started talking so quickly now that Sopeap could catch only about half the words. Something about a pair (as in a couple, or a fruit?), and leather, and a long word that **cropped up** again and again: apple stories? She tried to remember the sound, so that she could try looking it up **in her English-Khmer dictionary**, but she knew from past experience that unless she could get it down in writing, she probably wouldn't be able to find it, even with a spell checker.

Finally he stopped and looked at her questioningly. "Think you could do all that?" he asked.

She took a deep breath. "No problem," she said. She had long since discovered that it was easier to promise people anything they wanted first, and only afterward figure out what it was, and then do it. That was one of the

....

redone fixed

cropped up he said

in her English-Khmer dictionary in a dictionary that gave English words and meanings in the Cambodian language

ways her father's furniture repair store had survived at all.

Thomas flashed her a bright smile, the kind that people selling toothpaste on TV had, with such absolute confidence in the shiny **symmetry** of their teeth that they didn't have to think about them. "Great," he said. "And could you have it done by Christmas?"

Christmas was less than two months away. *Whatever it is he wants done to that chair,* Sopeap thought, we can do it by then. She nodded.

"And . . . could you **give me an estimate of how much** it would cost?"

She caught the familiar "how much" amid the swirl of other sounds, and smiled. Now she could start figuring out what he wanted. "Let's **work on a breakdown**," she said smoothly, "a breakdown of the costs." She liked compound words like *breakdown* and *armchair,* words that had an inner logic to them. It made them easy to remember.

She pulled out a pad and wrote on it: 12/25. "Christmas," she noted, then nonchalantly handed Tom the pencil. "Write down," she said, "what you want for your armchair."

....

symmetry straightness

give me an estimate of how much tell me how much you think

work on a breakdown make a list of how much each part costs

"But . . . " *But I just told you*, he probably started to say, but **restrained** himself. Instead, he started writing down a list of things, obligingly reading each word aloud as he wrote it.

"One: replace stuffing. Two: replace upholstery." So it wasn't "apple story," she noted. "Three: repair and polish wood."

As Tom was writing, Sopeap's father came through the swinging door, wiping his hands on a paint-splattered rag. He smelled of **turpentine**, and his hair was ruffled, sticking up in tufts. Thomas looked up at him and blinked. For the first time, Sopeap wished her father were somehow different—not as messy or casual. She tried to imagine him in a coat and tie, hair neatly slicked back, and couldn't.

"What does he want?" Duoc Phan asked, **his Cambodian sounding throaty and guttural**.

"To make the chair look new," Sopeap said, half guessing.

Mr. Phan **cast an experienced eye on it**. "The leather's all cracked. Does he want new leather?"

....

restrained stopped

turpentine paint remover

his Cambodian sounding throaty and guttural the Cambodian words sounding rough

cast an experienced eye on it looked at the chair

Sopeap looked over Tom's shoulder at the yellow pad and saw with relief that his handwriting was clear and precise. *U-p-h-o-l-s-t-e-r-y,* she memorized silently, and flipped open her dictionary. Yep, it meant what she thought it did: the covering for furniture. "Yes," she told her father, "he wants it replaced."

"It's not easy to get green leather," Mr. Phan said. "And such an ugly color. Why not use brown, or black?"

"You want another color?" Sopeap asked Tom hopefully.

Thomas shook his head, his red curls **bobbing** like tiny springs.

Mr. Phan understood the gesture, and disapproved. "That'll take a lot more time," he said. "Three months, at least."

Sopeap **dutifully translated this.**

Tom's curls stopped bouncing. His smile faded. "But you said you could have it by Christmas," he said.

"Replacing the leather," Sopeap said, "it takes much work."

....

bobbing moving

dutifully translated this told Tom what her father said

Tom's curls stopped bouncing. Tom stopped nodding his head.

His eyes were dark green, like prize jade. "The idea was to give it to my dad for a Christmas present," he said gruffly. "He misses Granddad even more than I do."

"Tell him it'd be cheaper to buy another chair," Phan said.

"It's special—this chair," Tom said, as if he understood Khmer. "**Been in the family** for . . . forever. I thought having it there, all new for Christmas, would be almost like having Granddad around still." Awkwardly, Tom poked at the outline of a spring that was jutting out from underneath the leather.

"All right, Christmas," Sopeap said. *Even if I have to spend hours helping Pa with it myself,* she vowed.

And it was as if the sun had suddenly come out again, the bright smile aglow beneath that red haze. "Hey, thanks!" he said. "It means a lot to me. Really!" With an impulsive tug, he grabbed Mr. Phan's hand and squeezed it. Quickly, Sopeap put her hands behind her back in case Tom should reach out for hers, too.

Been in the family My family has owned it

But he only smiled at her, stroking the top of the chair, running his hand lightly back and forth over the cracked leather. "Right by the fireplace, this armchair used to be. Nobody was allowed to use it, but he'd let me sit in his lap."

BEFORE YOU MOVE ON...

1. **Inference** What do you learn about Sopeap from her thoughts? Why didn't she say them out loud?

2. **Character** Reread pages 97 and 101–102. Why was the armchair important to Tom? What does this tell you about him?

LOOK AHEAD Read to page 113 to find out more of Sopeap's memories of "home."

Those words stayed with Sopeap and **ran through her mind** whenever she helped her father work on that chair. She imagined Thomas as a little boy, his jade-green eyes the same shade as the leather as he nestled in his grandfather's lap, listening to the rustling of the newspaper. As Sopeap carefully pried off each brass tack, careful not to rip the worn leather underneath so that her father could use it for a pattern later, she found herself wondering if the armchair used to sit under a standing lamp, and what the rest of the house was like. By the time she and her father had pulled off the leather, uncovering the cushion of horsehair and coiled springs underneath, she had developed a vivid image not only of a little Thomas, his hair catching the glint of the flames in the fireplace, but of the whole household, of how every chair and table and lamp had its own permanent place in a big old house that was so deeply comforting because nothing ever changed in it.

At the same time, she **suppressed** memories of her own house back in Cambodia, **how abruptly it had been abandoned**, clothes strewn on the floor, chairs overturned, books and photographs scattered everywhere

....

ran through her mind she remembered what Thomas said
suppressed tried not to think about
how abruptly it had been abandoned how quickly they left the house

in their haste to pack up the essentials and leave. They had been able to take so little with them—some bags of rice, some clothes, a few pieces of jewelry—but even that had either been used up during the harsh years of Communist rule or bartered away in the refugee camps on the Thai-Cambodian border afterward. **Against all odds, they still had each other, a semblance of a family**—and they had counted themselves incredibly lucky to have survived, found each other, and made it to America. The thought that they might have carried out a big armchair with them, into this new life, would have been **unthinkable, even ludicrous**.

Despite herself, Sopeap smiled at the image of an armchair like this one, being carried on her back, into the desolation of the refugee camps.

"What's so funny?"

Startled, Sopeap looked up at the figure who had slipped in through the doorway. It was Tom, silhouetted against the orange glow of the street light.

"Just thought I'd **drop in**, to see how it was going," he explained, stepping into the room uncertainly. "I mean,

....

Against all odds, they still had each other, a semblance of a family After all the difficult times, her family was still together

unthinkable, even ludicrous impossible, silly

drop in come to see you

Christmas is coming up, and . . . "

"And you think your armchair's not going to be ready," Sopeap finished for him, noting the disappointment in his face when he saw how unfinished the chair looked.

"Maybe I . . . I could help, if that will **speed things up**," he said.

"Maybe," Sopeap said. "But please, shut the door first." A heavy snow was falling outside, and a blast of cold wind was coming through the open doorway. Barely November, and already it felt as if the world were dead, its warmth and color all leached out into this muffled white stuff. Sopeap stood up.

"You don't like winter, do you?" he said, shutting the heavy door behind him.

"Not used to it," she said. Seven winters now, she had lived through—almost half her lifetime—yet she had never really gotten used to it.

"Do you miss . . . like, home?" He persisted. "You know . . . where you came from?"

She shrugged. Such a wonderful gesture, that American shrug. It could mean anything, everything, nothing. And it meant that she did not have to try to **put into words** all the swirl of feelings that thinking about

....

speed things up help make the chair ready faster
put into words talk about

"home" **brought to the surface**.

Hearing voices, Sopeap's father came out from the back room. In his hands were the new sheet of green leather and a pair of scissors. If he was surprised to see Thomas there, he showed no sign of it.

"We'll cut the leather today," he announced in Khmer.

"Is it okay if I watch, sir?" Tom asked in English.

"Fine with me," Mr. Phan replied in Khmer.

Sopeap watched this interchange in silence. She knew that her father understood very little English, and Tom even less Khmer, and yet here they were, **communicating amiably**.

Together she and Tom helped hold down the old piece of leather against the new, as Mr. Phan traced the outline of it with a piece of chalk. They held the new leather **taut** as he started slicing into it. Then, as he began fitting the new leather over the contours of the old armchair and nailing it onto the wood frame of the chair, Tom **spoke up**.

"Could I help do some nailing, too?" he asked.

"Go ahead," Mr. Phan said in Khmer, and handed over

···

brought to the surface made her feel
communicating amiably talking like friends
taut tightly
spoke up asked a question

his hammer. To Sopeap's surprise, Tom proved to be quite **adept** at it, nailing each tack squarely on the head.

"I spent whole summers reshingling our beach house," he said to her, **by way of explanation**.

It was getting dark, and outside the streetlights came on. The bright glow of the one just outside their shop illuminated the circle of snowflakes swirling around it, so that it almost looked like a full moon rising. Underneath, a few empty garbage cans lay on their sides in the gray slush. Mr. Phan turned and passed another hammer to Sopeap, and watched as she started to nail in the brass tacks alongside of Tom.

After a while her father **slipped off**, leaving just the two of them to continue working on the armchair by themselves. It was easy to talk, with the rhythmic hammering between them pacing their speech. Tom talked about his grandfather, how he had taken him for walks on the outskirts of Utica, along the Erie Canal towpath, and told him stories about his own grandfather having come from Ireland all the way to Upstate New York to join the army of young men digging the canal there.

"What about your grandparents?" he asked. "Did they

....

adept good
by way of explanation to explain why he was so good
slipped off went away

do fun things with you when you were a little girl?"

For a moment, Sopeap considered shrugging again, but **that seemed somehow disrespectful to the memory of her elders**.

Awkwardly, Sopeap started talking about how her grandmother used to make coconut cakes as a treat, "especially after I had practiced my dancing," she added, smiling at the memory.

"You danced?" Tom asked. "Like, how?"

"Like . . . this." In one fluid motion, Sopeap **swept** back the fingers of her right hand and extended her elbow far back. "That means a leaf," she said, "and this means a flower." She pressed her thumb and index finger together, fanning out the other three. Then, twisting the hand upside down, and arching all her fingers back again to the Kbach Sung Luc position, she grinned and said teasingly, "Together that means 'Come here.'"

The flicker of interest in Tom's eyes excited and scared her. Quickly, she stepped back and held her arm out, hand in yet another position, with all fingers touching except for the index, which pointed straight up.

....

that seemed somehow disrespectful to the memory of her elders she did not want to insult her ancestors

swept moved

The flicker of interest in Tom's eyes Tom seemed interested and that

She hoped it would look like *Stop!* even though she knew it only symbolized a bud or sprout.

"Cool," Tom said.

"But my fingers . . . " she said, bending them back with her other hand, "like sticks." *Instead of like lotus stalks*, she wanted to say, but didn't know how. They used to be so supple, she could flex them all the way back into a curve, but they didn't bend back nearly as far now.

"I should practice," she said. "My grandma will **scold me big-time** when she sees me so stiff."

"Your grandma's around?" Tom asked. Sopeap thought **she detected a hint of envy in his voice**.

"Not around here," she said with a laugh. "She's back . . . home, in Cambodia. But maybe she will come to visit, or stay with us."

"That's great. When?"

"Next year, maybe. We started **the paperwork for her** long ago."

"Hope it'll be in the spring or summer," Tom said. "She'd probably hate the winter even more than you do!"

"She won't mind," Sopeap said. "My grandma's . . . " She tried to think of the right word. Picking up a scrap of

....

scold me big-time yell at me

she detected a hint of envy in his voice he sounded jealous

the paperwork for her to fill out papers so she could come to the United States

the green leather from the armchair, Sopeap stretched it taut. "She's like this . . . cannot tear," she said.

Tom nodded. "Tough," he said. "Leathery. My granddad was like that, too."

Leathery. Sopeap **filed the word away**. She remembered how the skin on her grandmother's face was like old leather, **parched** and sagging unless it was pulled taut by her quick, radiant smiles. How hard Sopeap had tried when she was a little girl to earn one of those smiles. Those long afternoons spent in the dance pavilion inside the palace, standing in line behind the older girls, trying to move just the way they did—bending her knees and flexing her ankles in slow, fluid steps. And like a mother hawk over her **fledglings**, her grandmother had watched them all, sternly correcting a posture here, a movement there. Once in a great while, when they had completed a particularly hard series of steps gracefully, she would flash them that lovely smile.

Sopeap tried to describe this to Tom, at first **haltingly and then with growing ease**, as both the memories and the English words flowed from her.

....

filed the word away tried to remember that word

parched dry

fledglings babies

haltingly and then with growing ease slowly and then more comfortably

"She sounds nice," Tom said.

"Except when she was . . . tough." Sopeap laughed. "She used to bend my fingers back so much, it really hurt." Sopeap demonstrated, flexing the fingers of her right hand back with her left, bending them so far back that her fingertips almost touched the back of her wrist. Her knuckles cracked, and she grimaced with pain.

"They are so stiff now, my fingers. I haven't practiced enough." Still, she showed him some of the basic hand gestures, or *kbach*, that **symbolized** a flower, a bud, and a leaf.

"My grandma will scold me, for sure, when she sees how stiff my fingers have become," Sopeap said. "She wanted to train me, to dance the part of Sita—Rama's beautiful wife, who gets kidnapped by a demon. It's from *The Reamker*, a very old story that came to Cambodia from India thousands of years ago."

"Awesome," Tom said obligingly. "Can you dance that part, then?"

"I was learning it from my grandmother when . . . when . . . " Sopeap paused. Were there words, in any language, to describe what happened after the Communists took power in Cambodia? She shrugged.

....

symbolized looked like

Tom did not **press her for details**. "You should start practicing again," he said.

"Yeh, or my grandmother will get angry and take my hands and do this." With one hand, Sopeap bent the fingers of her other hand so far back that the joints and knuckles on it all made loud cracking sounds. "She wanted me to do that dance like, perfect, real bad. Always it was practice, practice, practice."

"Why don't you, then?"

Again the shrug. No music, no costumes, no monsoon rains—how could she ever hope to re-create the magic and perfection of that dance? **It was no use to even try.** Sopeap sighed. "No use," she said. Then, because that sounded so lame, she added, "Too much homework, maybe."

An easy excuse, one **within the realm of Tom's experience**. He groaned in sympathy. "Like those quadratic equations due tomorrow? They're hard."

"No, they're not," Sopeap said. Numbers and algebraic symbols were simple, compared to slippery words. "You want to do them together?"

....

press her for details ask what happened

It was no use to even try. She could never do it.

within the realm of Tom's experience that Tom could understand

And so **an understanding of sorts was developed**. Sopeap would help Tom with the algebra homework, and he would proofread her assignments for history or English. And together they would work on the armchair, rushing to try to get it finished in time for Christmas.

Sometimes, as a study break, they would play the city-building game together, taking turns being mayor as they extended the subway system or upgraded to a newer nuclear power plant. Sopeap's computer was an old one, its hard disk straining to absorb the graphics-rich game. It took so long to load the game that after a few sessions Thomas brought along **his laptop**, and they installed the software and downloaded their saved game into it. As they switched over and started playing on Thomas's laptop, Sopeap thanked him.

He grinned. "**It's the software that's the important part**," he said. "You can always switch the hardware, but it's that fantastic city we're building that counts."

....

an understanding of sorts was developed they started to help each other

his laptop a smaller computer

It's the software that's the important part It doesn't matter that your computer is old —the game disk is what is important

BEFORE YOU MOVE ON...

1. **Inference** Why didn't Sopeap like to think or talk about "home"?

2. **Character** Describe Sopeap's grandmother. How do you know that Sopeap loved her?

LOOK AHEAD Read pages 114–120 to find out what happens when Sopeap's family gets a letter from Cambodia.

The **bleak** winter days slipped by, each one shorter than the day before, and before they knew it, Christmas was only a week away. Fretting about whether the armchair would be fully ready in time for Christmas, Thomas took to coming to the shop even more often. Sometimes they would ride the same bus from school, chatting as they walked down the **grimy** sidewalks. By the time they reached the storefront, it would already be dark, and the streetlights would be glowing like a row of eerie full moons.

Late one afternoon, when it was snowing hard, Sopeap and Tom walked from the bus stop together and pushed open the heavy door to the woodworking shop.

The room was cold, and shrouded in darkness. Sopeap turned on the light and was startled to see her father by the window, just standing there, staring out at the snow. Behind him was the green armchair, its legs sanded and newly varnished.

"Pa?" Sopeap said, uncertain.

"Turn off the light," he **snapped at her** in Khmer.

She turned it off. In the dusk, the glow of the streetlight outside radiated outward.

....

bleak dark, cold
grimy dirty
snapped at her said angrily

"Mr. Phan," Thomas said. "You okay?"

"The armchair is finished," Phan said **curtly**. "Tell him to take it away and get out of here!"

Sopeap was so stunned that she did not know how to respond. She had often **sensed a reticence on her father's part toward Tom,** almost a disapproval at their growing friendship, but he had never **displayed such overt hostility at** him before.

Before she could say anything, her father strode across the room and shoved his way past them, slamming the door behind him.

In the silence that followed, Thomas went over to where Mr. Phan had been standing and picked up the long white envelope that he had dropped there. Silently he held it out to Sopeap.

Even before she saw the neat lines of Khmer script on the return address, she knew what it was: a letter from Cambodia. And even before she took it over to read by the light of the streetlamp outside, she knew what it would say. Her grandmother would not be visiting them, not this spring or summer. Or any other time. Not now, not ever. Never.

....

curtly quickly, angrily

sensed a reticence on her father's part toward Tom,
thought her father did not like Tom and there was

displayed such overt hostility at been mean to

Shakily, Sopeap walked over to the armchair and steadied herself against it. Her grandmother was old, her health hadn't been good, she might not even have liked America. Dully, Sopeap started stroking the green leather on the armrest.

Back and forth, back and forth, her fingers slid so hard against the leather that it hurt her palms. *Don't think, don't feel, don't remember, it's all right, it's all right. It's all right, it's all right,* back and forth. The leather was smooth and solid under her hands. But the memories came anyway, **seeping out over the edge of her consciousness** like moonlight from behind clouds. Her grandmother sweeping away leaves from the doorstep with an old broom, one arm held behind her back. Or sitting under the lamplight, sharpening pencils with a rusty old knife as Sopeap did her homework. Or watching **intently**, while Sopeap practiced her dance gestures.

I should have practiced, Sopeap told her grandmother. *I should have practiced the dancing.*

"Sopeap . . . I just . . . I'm sorry . . . " It was Tom, **hovering nearby**. "I mean, in a way, she isn't really gone. They're still there . . . somehow."

....

seeping out over the edge of her consciousness coming to her slowly

intently seriously

hovering nearby standing close to her

Sopeap bit down on her lips. *Easy for you to say, she thought bitterly. You with your family living in the same area for **generations**. You with the same furniture and the same house and the same friends who knew all of you from years and years back. You've got everything you need right here to help you relive and remember. You've managed to hold on to something of the dead, the past. You can even sit in the same old armchair they did.*

But she said nothing. She didn't even try to shrug.

Awkwardly, Tom put his hand on hers and tried to lift it off the armrest. She felt the sting of tears and gripped the armrest even more tightly.

But gently, patiently, Tom worked her fingers loose, until he had her palm held flat between both of his.

Then he did a strange thing. Just as gently and patiently, he pressed her fingers backward, arching them back so far it almost hurt.

Suddenly she understood: it was the Kbach Sung Luc, one of the basic gestures of Cambodian classical dance. He had remembered it from that afternoon when she had told him about her grandmother, and how she had taught Sopeap to dance. *She may be gone*, he was telling her now, but **what she taught you has been passed on to you**.

....

generations *many years*
what she taught you has been passed on to you *you will always remember what she taught you*

"Like software," Sopeap murmured.

Tom let go of her hand. "Even better," he said. **"It's shareware."**

He's right, Sopeap thought. *What I have can never— and should never be—copyrighted. What has been passed on to me is harder than any hardware, softer than any software. A series of words, a sequence of movements—a story, a dance, these things Grandma passed on to me, these things that are almost sacred in their simplicity. And they are mine, yet they belong to me only as much as the flame of a candle belongs to its wick. When the candle is melted away, the flame is passed on—that's all.*

She watched as Tom gave her a reassuring nod before walking out the door, taking just one backward glance at her before he disappeared into the darkness beyond the streetlight.

It was still snowing, the wet streaks of snow around the streetlamp like slivers of sunlight through the trees around the dance pavilion. Through her tears, Sopeap squinted at the lamplight outside, and **borne by a wave of longing so strong** that she felt herself transported back to a twilight under the pavilion, she could almost sense her

....

"It's shareware." "It's something that many people can use and share together."

borne by a wave of longing so strong wanting to see her grandmother so much

grandmother behind her, watching.

And so, without allowing herself to think too much about it, Sopeap started to dance for her grandmother. At first awkwardly, and then with more grace, as if her whole body was moving **with a will of its own**, she practiced her dance steps. Gradually, and so naturally that she couldn't tell whether she was remembering or making up the dance steps, she danced within a play of light and shadow.

And as she danced, Sopeap felt as if her grandmother was right there, watching her, perhaps even sitting in the green armchair. But she did not dare look, for fear that **this tenuous sense of her grandmother would vanish** if she did.

Teach me, she asked her grandmother silently. And sure enough, when she realized she was not **holding her back erect** enough, she could almost feel the firm pressure of her grandmother's hands against her shoulder blades, spreading them back. And so Sopeap strained, with fierce concentration, to move correctly, in exactly the same way that her grandmother had taught her to move. Slowly she could feel her **limbs** loosening up, her movements

....

with a will of its own without thinking about it
this tenuous sense of her grandmother would vanish she would not feel like her grandmother was there anymore
holding her back erect standing straight
limbs arms and legs

becoming more certain and graceful.

I know I'm not good enough for you, she told her grandmother. *But I will practice, really I will. I will **track down** a tape of the music; I will find another classical dance teacher to train me; I will remember and relearn what you had passed on to me, Grandma. You'll see.*

There—it was done. Not perfectly, not even close to perfectly, but she had danced it as best as she could. She let the fluid discipline of the dance movements guide her body, and as she performed the last few movements, she knew that she had danced with enough grace and symmetry that her grandmother would have approved. Solemnly, she lowered her arms, then stopped.

Impulsively, she turned around, wanting to see her grandmother's radiant smile.

There was nothing there. The green armchair stood in the middle of the room, stark and silent. Beyond it, outside the doorway, was the streetlamp, **haloed** by a swirl of snowflakes. A thick white blanket of snow had **built up** and was draped over the upturned garbage cans and empty bottles strewn on the sidewalk.

Sopeap took a deep breath, and sat down on the armchair.

....

track down find
haloed circled
built up fallen

BEFORE YOU MOVE ON...

1. **Plot** What changed after Sopeap read the letter?
2. **Conclusions** What did Tom help Sopeap to understand?